When Blood 1

A Bad Date Forensic

By

Richard DeVall

COPYRIGHT

OTHER TITLES
BY RICHARD DEVALL

ABOUT THIS BOOK

This story begins with a supercharged lift-off, and doesn't stop until the end.

Soon after meeting Steven Porowski from a dating site, Wendy is disturbed enough by his behavior to exit the restaurant where they were having dinner. Before driving away, Steven threatens her, and not long after that threat, he follows through with a flurry of mind-boggling technical and physical episodes.

Wendy and her sister, Jennifer, recruit Wendy's brother-in-law, Hunter, to help with Porowski, and he becomes Steven's latest victim. The police charge Hunter with the disappearance and murder of Porowski.

Ultimately, it comes down to two sisters and their mother to find Porowski, and rescue his kidnapped victim.

Sprinkled with humor and wit, this cat and mouse game with a psychopath ends on a high note, and leaves the reader to imagine a future that's both dark and light.

Chapter 1

Wendy felt there was something off about Steven. She moved the food on her plate around with her fork as she listened to him talk. There was a scale, a sense of balance a person has, a perception of another's view of their self-worth. It moved and weaved in between doubt, and confidence. She was picking up that there was something amiss. Online, he'd been confident, and able to carry on a conversation. He'd shown a bit of wit and humor when they'd chatted. But now, he didn't hold her eye. He glanced around here and there, but mostly down at his plate. His eyes seemed too close, giving his face a slightly pinched look. It wasn't something she noticed when they first met, when they had an awkward hug. It was a learned observation as her nerves settled, and she was able to move beyond her self-consciousness. Then came the inevitable, and annoying comparison, to Ray.

Tonight, it was her first date with Steven from the dating app City Singles. When he walked into the restaurant, he glanced around. Her first impression was handsome, and he looked like the photo he had on the dating site, which was a relief. She didn't register anything off about his symmetry because everything was where it should be. It was only after he was close, and she had time to study him, that she saw his eyes were a touch too close.

"How's your food?" he asked after they'd been served, and had some small talk.

She looked at her plate as if it were an afterthought, almost surprised. "It's good." She took in a mouthful of fried Brussel sprout quarter as if to prove her point.

Steven made a show of adjusting his seat, then leaned forward. "Ever wonder about the person that invented the rocking chair?" It was rhetorical, so he continued. "I mean, what happened? Suddenly they said, 'I'm sick of sitting in a chair that doesn't move.'"

"I think it came about from women rocking babies to sleep, or maybe breastfeeding," Wendy offered.

"Well, Wendy," he replied, his eyes only catching hers for a brief moment, "that makes more sense than anything I was thinking." He seemed a little depleted because she didn't join in on his lame observation, or question.

The restaurant's volume was increasing. There were plates being scraped, glasses were clinking, and voices were filling the air. A large group, possibly an extended family, from the far corner, broadcast waves of sudden laughter. Wendy smiled at Steven after each outburst. It was contagious, this happy group erupting with laughter in the corner. Even their waitress was laughing. But Steven seemed oblivious, and it made Wendy think about something she'd read recently about yawns and involuntary responses among humans, and primates. It was a study of autism, and she wondered if Steven had some subtle form of the neurological condition. She couldn't ask, but she was forming an opinion.

She reached conclusions about people too soon. There was an intuitive leap to process their choice of clothing, and dissect every sentence. Dwelling on things had become a problem in past relationships. She took work home, every look and comment replayed for hours, tormenting her thoughts. It interfered with her sleep. She ended up seeing Dr. Lyons, and the good doctor prescribed Zoloft, a serotonin reuptake inhibitor. A standard depression medicine that, among other things, shut down excessive rumination. It was a Godsend to Wendy, and it made her much happier, but it titled her into becoming something that her Mother referred to as having '*The ten-cent-psychologist syndrome*'.

"*What's your ten-cent take on your date?*" She could already hear her Mother ask that tomorrow when they had their Saturday morning talk. She wondered about the answer. He was dressed nicely, and smelled good. The guy is handsome in a kind of detached way, but he glances at her, and doesn't hold her eye. It's as if he's riddled with guilt, or shyness, and not wanting her to read something inside of him. This thought process made her realize she wasn't eager for a second date. She wanted someone familiar with social norms; she needed that to keep herself balanced. His weirdness was tugging on her insecurities.

"You're prettier in person compared to your photo. I mean, it's a nice surprise to tell you the truth. So many people post these glamour shots from ten years ago."

"Well, thank you, Steven. I was relieved to see that you weren't some middle-aged man in the throes of a divorce posting a picture from his college days," Wendy smiled.

"Do people still do that? I mean, it's going to catch up with them as soon they meet in person," Steven asked.

"I think, for the most part, people are honest, but I've been on a few of these dates where the picture they post is from a few years back, and several pounds ago," Wendy said.

"You're my third date in the past five years, Wendy. After my first online date, the girl, Abigail, well, she and I became exclusive for three years. We almost got married. We lived with each other for the last two years." Steven turned his eyes sideways and looked toward the kitchen area. He seemed fixated on the two stainless steel swinging doors to the left of the bar. "What happened still bothers me. We were not just lovers, but best friends."

"And your second date?" Wendy asked.

"My second date," he smiled, and held her eyes a little bit longer than a glance. "It was horrible, and I felt drained after it ended. I'm not overly sensitive, but she accused me of having an online personality and joking around, then this serious person shows up for the date. I was tired from work. She told me she was sick of meeting men that weren't comfortable in their own skin."

"Oh, my God," Wendy said. "What a terrible experience."

"It wasn't an ego booster. I remember thinking about how bad the evening went, and that I had to pay for everything. The lady drank a lot of wine, and ordered the most expensive items on the menu. Looking back, I think she hates men, or one in particular, and lets that experience spill over to all men."

"That's probably true," Wendy said.

She remembered his page read he was 34-years-old. Steven looked a bit younger, being the right weight, and he didn't smoke, and was yet to finish his first glass of wine. He probably has some healthy habits. A fleeting image of the last walk she and Ray had flashed in her mind. "I guess there are all kinds out there. I hope you didn't let her get into your head, Steven."

"Honestly, she sent me back into my shell. So, you're my third date." He flicked his wrist as if dismissing something. "I hope it's going okay for you."

Maybe he wasn't some offshoot spectrum of autism, or a rapid cycling manic-depressive. Perhaps he was just shy, and that was endearing to Wendy. It tipped Steven into the cute department. "It's going fine for me. You seem a bit shy."

"I spend too much time by myself, and when I'm around people, I feel like an intruder. It takes me a while to get comfortable."

"Why do you spend so much time by yourself?"

"It's my job," Steven answered. "I do security checks for several companies from my office, and also from my home. I monitor them, install updates, things like that. It's my own business."

"Oh, you're an IT guy?"

"Yes," he said.

Wendy began to feel more comfortable with Steven, and as that happened, she started tasting the food; it was outstanding. He'd picked a superb restaurant. "What happened with you and Abigail, Steven?"

He looked at her, and held her gaze a little longer than some of his earlier nervous glances. "She developed incurable brain cancer, and lived eight months after her diagnosis."

"Oh, my God," she gasped as her hand flew up to her mouth. "I'm so sorry I brought it up."

Steven nodded, and shifted some of his salmon around on his plate with his knife. "The sting of it is over, Wendy, but I don't want to talk about it if that's alright."

"Of course." *Well, you stepped into it that one.* "This swordfish is out of this world; the portion is more than I'm used to," she remarked as she tried to change the subject.

He leaned forward. "I don't like to leave a restaurant hungry. It's one of my pet peeves."

He cleared his throat, then added, "I also don't like women who pry." He gave Wendy a stern glance as if he was teaching her the rules of how their relationship would move forward.

Wendy set her fork down. She stared at Steven for a moment. Was that hurt, or anger? Either way, she saw nothing but red flags. She picked up a cloth napkin, dabbed her lips, then put it back on the table. She turned to her left, and grabbed her purse from the extra chair. "I'm no longer comfortable, Steven. Please don't follow me to my car, or contact me again." With that, Wendy stood up and walked out of the restaurant unhurried; she was not the kind of person to cause a scene. Once she crossed the threshold, and her foot landed on the sidewalk, she broke into a sprint, and jogged to her car.

Her hand was shaking when her key slipped into the ignition. Steven jerked the driver's door open, and yelled at her. "All I said was I don't like it when a woman pries and digs." His teeth were showing as if he was a rabid animal. "And you wouldn't leave good enough alone.

You had to open a wound, then you leave me at the table bleeding. Well, I won't stand for it, you'll see." Steven pointed his index finger at her, and held it a couple of inches from her face. "You just wait." After those final words, Steven was done yelling. He spun around, and walked away.

Chapter 2

Wendy was still shaking when she entered her townhome complex, and parked in the number 19 space allotted for her car. Occasionally on Friday nights, one of her neighbors would have a party, and when that happened, she had to park a long way from her entrance door. Thank God for small favors; it wasn't a good night to traipse across the asphalt. She wanted to barricade herself behind a locked door, and remove all her information on the City Singles web site. *What a freak that guy Steven turned out to be. He went from a shy man to an aggressive asshole in about one minute.*

Her phone chirped, and she jumped. It was her mother calling. She probably forgot that Wendy had a date. "Hi, Mom."

Her Mother spoke very quietly, in a hushed tone. "Hi, sweety, I want you to come over here tomorrow morning, and find out what's going on with Jennifer."

Wendy looked in her review mirror, watching a car with a couple in it drive passed her parked car. "Why, what's going on?"

"Jenny's moved in with the kids. She won't talk to me about her and Hunter."

"Oh, shit," Wendy said, "that doesn't sound good."

"No, it doesn't," her mom replied. "Come over and see your niece and nephew. Start digging, and tell me what's going on, alright?"

"I'll be there early tomorrow, mom."

Her mother asked, "How was your date? You're home early."

"It was a nightmare, mom. He grabbed my car door, swung it open, and yelled and screamed at me." Wendy tried not to become emotional. She couldn't believe she was breaking down on the phone with her Mother.

"Come here, right now; you don't need to be by yourself tonight."

Wendy sniffed. "I'll be there in ten minutes. I'm still in my car."

On the ride to her mother's house, Wendy thought about her sister, and the children. Something awful must have happened with her husband, Hunter, for Jenny to have uprooted everyone, and flee to her mom's house. Did Hunter cheat on her? Did he turn violent? The man is substantial, size-wise, and since they've been married, he's gained more muscle. She knows he works out. So does Jenny, for that matter.

Wendy is four years younger than her sister. Jenny is 34, and Wendy hit 30 a month earlier. A lot of her friends have kids, and a big house in the suburbs. She's felt, at times, like the romance pixie-dust was sprinkled on all of her friends, and missed her. She knows she's attractive. Every boss she'd ever had had hit on her. That's one of the reasons she didn't stay at any job for years, until she started working for Loraine. Now she's in management, and loves her job. It can be all-consuming, at times, like when there are big projects, and a deadline. She can't imagine having to keep a husband content, and raising children. Not at this stage of her life.

But then there were lonely nights, and evenings, like the one she'd just experienced with a horrible date from an online dating site. At times like this, she felt drenched in loser dust, and it made her have images of a solitaire future where her expectations were a glass of wine, and a book for the weekend. In that vision, there may be a cat, or a dog, lingering around somewhere nearby. For now, she couldn't handle a pet. She killed house plants. And, there were times when she flung open her refrigerator to be shocked that there was no food inside the box. She'd end up shopping at nine in the evening, and by the time she'd unloaded everything, she was too tired to eat.

So why did she go on dates? Because she had hope, and still considered herself young. A subjective stance, but she felt youthful most of the time. She had needs that weren't always quieted with Mister Buzz in the box tucked deep inside her bedside table. Her dream guy would be as busy as her at his job. What little time they had together would be filled with intense lovemaking, and short vacations to exotic places.

She parked behind her sister's minivan. A worn sticker on its bumper read, *My son attends Slate Shore Elementary.* Wendy scrambled up the terraced steps from the street toward the porch light. She rang the bell, and thought she heard a distant foghorn blow from Madden's Inlet. She noticed the air had a slight chill, accompanied by moisture beginning to collect on the wrought iron handrail. Fall was coming. The maple trees were turning color, the giant oak trees in Slate Shore seemed oblivious to the dying light, and colder air. Their leaves were dark green, and yet to show any sign of change.

The door flew open, and a warm gust of air covered Wendy. Her mom gathered her into a deep hug that made Wendy feel loved. Her mother was her best friend, and often an excellent sounding board to bounce some of her misconceptions, and conclusions. So, she respected her mother, and used her for her guidance and emotional support. Wendy had known only love as she grew up in this grand old house, and she missed her father dearly. He was taken too soon by a heart attack that had devastated all of them. Though her mother could be stoic and reserved, she had leaned heavily on both of her daughters in those early days. That was almost four years ago, and the sting of it had lost some of its bite.

Beverly patted her daughter's back, and said very softly, "Don't forget to find out what happened with Jen."

Wendy caught her mother's eye when they separated, and she nodded. If Jen didn't want her mother to know something, there was a reason, and Wendy wouldn't rat out her sister. She saw her niece in her pajamas curled up in her sister's lap on a Camila Loveseat. Wendy removed her sweater. Her mother kept the house at the same temperature as the warm setting on an oven. She felt slightly cooked whenever she visited. She smiled at Jenny, and collapsed in front of Olivia. "Hi, sweetie, can you give your Aunt Wendy a hug?"

The little girl smiled with her cherub face, and stuck her arms out. Wendy adored her. She gave her a big hug and said, "Why aren't you in bed and asleep?" Olivia shrugged. Wendy looked at Jen. "Is she sleeping in the second spare, or first?"

Jen said, "Room number one."

"Come on, big girl, I'll tuck you in, and make sure there are only angels with lollipops hiding in the closet, and under the bed. How does that sound?"

Olivia once again shrugged. Wendy scooped her up, and bounced her in her arms as she carried her back to the spare bedroom, tucked her in, and kissed her forehead. "Listen, angel, your mom and I need to talk grownup talk, so can you be a big girl, and go to sleep?"

"But you didn't check the closet, and under the bed," Olivia's eyes widened on her four-year-old face. Wendy saw the alarm, and sprang to her feet.

"I forgot, kid. I'll do that, right now." She walked funny to make Olivia giggle as she went to the closet, and opened the door. A smell of mothballs met her nose as she looked inside and saw her mom's funeral dress wrapped from the cleaners, and one pair of flat black shoes on the floor. She turned to Olivia. "I saw two angels licking lollipops in the back of the closet.

"No, you didn't," her niece smiled.

Wendy said, "One of them is named Tinker Bell, and the other one is named Socks."

"Socks," Olivia repeated.

"Yep, Socks, the angel; she's not from around here," she added as if that explained everything. Olivia seemed to accept that explanation, and yawned.

Wendy looked under the bed and declared, "All's clear, kid, nothing under the bed, not even an angel, although some might come later to make sure you have good dreams."

She pulled the door, leaving it slightly open to let a tiny bit of light filter into the room. She remembered doing that from the times when the kids stayed at her house. Then she walked into the living room, and sat across from Jen in her fathers' old recliner. "You look good, Jen. Did you do something different with your hair?"

"Stop the bullshit, Wen. I'm matronly, chubby, and a hideous bore," she smiled.

"I know that," Wendy said, "but did you do something different with your hair?"

"I think I washed it last month."

Wendy smiled. "It's bad, hum?"

"Yeah," Jenny started to get misty-eyed. "He's in love with Valerie Washington, his black secretary. What the fuck? I mean, it's not that she's black. Well, in a way, it is. I mean, how can you compete with a different race? He says he likes the contrasting colors." Her mouth hung open, but nothing came out.

"When did this happen?" Wendy asked.

Jenny waved an arm across the air. "I've known something was off for months. I mean, if he doesn't love me, okay, shit happens, but what about the kids? They need their dad, and he's like surprised I even brought them up. He's such a selfish pig."

"What a dick," Wendy said. Then she looked around the room as if searching for something. "Has mom got something to drink around here?"

"She's got some God-awful wine in a box in the cabinet above the toaster."

Her mother, who had skipped out of the room to check on Drake, her six-year-old grandson, came into the living room, and asked her two girls if they wanted some hot chocolate. "No, mom," Wendy answered. "We're going to drink your box of wine. Do you want a glass?"

"You're drinking the whole box?"

"Only if you help, mom."

"Alright, I'll get the glasses. You open the box, and pour."

Once everyone had a half-full glass of wine, Wendy asked Jen, once again. "What's different about your hair?"

"When Hunter told me he loved his secretary," she glanced at her mother, nodding, as if to say okay, now you know, "I went to the stylist, and got a new design. Then I got depressed, and didn't keep up with it. Now, what you're looking at, is an overgrown style that wasn't me to begin with."

Both Wendy, and her mom, at the same time, said, "I like it."

Jennifer smiled, and looked from her mother to her sister. "That's because you guys love me." She did all she could to fight back the tears. Then, she raised her glass as a toast to the two women in front of her. "This, too, shall pass," she said.

Wendy's phone pinged, and she glanced at it. There was a message from City Singles, the dating app she'd used to meet Steven. It read, *Your account is canceled for posting inappropriate, or sexually explicit material in direct violation of our policies.* Wendy was looking at a picture of herself wearing nothing, sprawled out on a couch. Her face was on someone else's body. Someone more voluptuous than herself. "Ut, oh, I've got a problem."

Chapter 3

In a perfect world, husbands wouldn't fall for their secretary, and dates wouldn't post doctored images on dating sites. Something in the back of Wendy's brain told her this situation with Steven wasn't over. She felt a hiccup in the universe; effervescent bubbles massaged her intuition, and essentially prepared her for more shenanigans. "He's crazy, and that means he's obsessive, compulsive, suffering from low self-esteem with anger issues, and a bunch of other shit."

After they all commented that the body wasn't Wendy's, they discussed safety options. An hour later, they'd moved on to smear unfaithful Hunter. Maybe it's a phase. Around two-thirty am, the big box of wine was empty. Wendy fell asleep on the couch. Her last thought was about a man named Ray; a man she thought she'd be spending the rest of her life with, instead of sleeping on an uncomfortable couch by herself. Jennifer shared her mothers' bed.

THE THREE WOMEN WERE depleted from last night's irreverent, and raucous behavior. Their conversation swelled and crashed, receded, and formed new, over, and over until it was nearing four in the morning. Wendy appeared to be mesmerized by the depth of the coffee inside the cup in front of her. Her thoughts were staggered, and weaved between slow waves of pain, and a rolling stomach. The kids were animated, and Jenny was dealing with them like a pro. Thank God, because

Wendy, and her mother, were near comatose. The hot temperature her mother insisted on keeping the house was baking Wendy, and made her shift in her chair as if its comfort was for others, not her.

"I feel like death warmed over," her mother said.

"You don't look too good, either, mom. I know about the warmed-over part. Do you not have any circulation in your body?"

Her mother stared at her for a moment, and internally seemed to check a rapid response. "I've told you before, sweetie. It's a thyroid condition."

"What the hell is this?" Jennifer yelled while staring at her laptop.

The women were sitting at a round table with claw feet, while the kids were in the dining room eating cereal, and playing games on their tablets. Jennifer turned the tablet around so the screen was facing her mother, and sister. In bold, colorful letters, stenciled over the face of a smiling clown, was written, "Hi Drake, I like Slate Shore Elementary, too."

"Who would be writing my son?"

Wendy said, "I think it's that creep, Steven."

"How would he know anything about Drake?'

"If he followed me here, which he must be an expert at hiding because I kept looking in my rearview mirror, then he would have read it on your bumper sticker; *My son goes to Slate Shore Elementary*."

Jennifer sat back, and looked at Wendy, then her mother. "Nobody messes with my kids, and I mean nobody."

Their mother said, "Are you sure it's him? I mean, that feels like a stretch."

"Only one way to find out," Jennifer said, thinking out loud. "I need to contact Hunter, and have him use an IT guy to check this stuff out. Maybe from there, we can cross-reference things, and find out if it's our little sicko."

Drake shouted from the dining room, "It's Aunt Wendy naked."

All three women ran into the dining room, and stared at Drake's tablet, which he plays Minecraft on for hours. There, filling up the screen, was the photoshopped image of Wendy with her legs slightly, seductively spread. It was the same picture Wendy saw from City Singles. "Well, there's no doubt about who it is, now."

"The only good thing about that," Jennifer said, "is that I don't have to call Hunter because now we know who's messing with my son."

Wendy deleted the page on the tablet. Back at the kitchen table, Beverly asked, "What's next? Should we call the police?"

"Shit," Wendy said. "I just deleted hard evidence of a pornographic nature sent to a child."

Jennifer began talking. "Mom, if you can watch the kids, we," she pointed back and forth between herself, and her sister, "can do a little surveillance on this guy, Steven, and maybe put the shoe on the other foot."

Wendy asked, "How are we going to find out where he lives? I don't even know his last name."

"You said he was on City Singles, and that he owned an IT business. Let's start with the dating site."

"They've kicked me off for my X-rated photo."

"I'll join," Jennifer said.

Soon, all three were bent over a laptop staring at a photo of Steven, and his profile.

"He's not a bad looking guy, Wen."

Their mother piped in. "I liked the man on the page before him; Michael."

Her daughters smiled, and Jenny recommended she join a site, and start dating. To the surprise of both girls, she said, "I was seriously thinking about it, but this situation with your disturbed man, Steven, has given me pause."

"You and me both, Mom," Wendy said.

As they studied Steven's photo, they zoomed in on his T-shirt that brandished a small logo on the left side. Jennifer used her touch screen to zoom in, and take a closer look. The letters were too blurry to read when she enlarged the screen. She slowly backed out, trying to find the sweet spot, and nothing seemed to work.

Her mother said, "Hold it right there. I'll be back in a minute."

Their mother returned with a magnifying glass, and put it over the image on the screen. They could read the words on the shirt; **Stealth Security** – 24/7 Observation and Protection. "Wow, Mom, your old school solution worked great."

Jennifer wrote the name down on a sheet of paper, and closed out the dating site. She googled the company, and immediately clicked on the web address. A slick video showed how Stealth Security could automatically flag anyone phishing for information. Furthermore, they installed firewalls, implemented updates, and even held an online tutorial for assessing security risks, and solutions. The only person shown on the website was Steven Porowski. The company's address, and phone number were displayed.

Jennifer moved off the website, and googled Steven Porowski. There was a surprising number of them in the United States. They soon whittled it down to the only one that could be their guy. Beverly paid the $18 to have all the public records of Porowski available to them. It was a treasure trove of information; where he went to college, and photos of him in high school. Wendy was getting excited. So were Beverly, and Jen.

"This is magically taking away some of my hangover," Wendy said.

"Same here," Jen confessed, then added, "let's go stalk this dude."

"Oh, my," their mother said. "You two aren't detectives. This man could be dangerous."

Jenny said, "Mom, we're just going to see this guy's place of work, and get some information on him. He's writing Drake, and I need to know everything I can about a man sending porn to your six-year-old grandson."

Beverly said, "Take your father's pistol just to be safe."

Jenny grinned like an escaped convict, and suddenly she and Wendy felt like bad-asses ready to double-tap the douche-bag known as Steven Porowski. Once in the still solitude of their mother's car, before Jennifer turned the key in the ignition, the two sisters looked at each other, and recognized a seriousness that hung in the air. It was nearly palpable; as thick as a sheet of waxed paper. Wendy broke the brief spell. "We have to take it slow, Jen. This guy may be homicidal."

They'd decided on their mother's car because Jenny's soccer van had the bumper sticker he'd used to track down Drake when he followed Wendy's Volkswagen. Their mother's Chevy Equinox was a luxury model, and comfortable, even luxurious. They adjusted the seats, and both were experiencing a lower back massage as they pulled away from her house on a vague mission to learn what they could about Steven.

"I want a burner phone," Jenny exclaimed.

"Of course, you do," Wendy said with a slight snort.

"I have this thing Hunter gave me that clips on my phone; it's a little telescope. I wanted it to take pictures of Drake when he played sports. I can zoom in from quite a distance. But if we were to send Steven a photo of himself, or anything else, I don't want it to come from my phone."

"Yeah, but if you send him photos, you have to get a pretty expensive phone. You'll need the internet, and all the stuff we have on our phones." They both had the latest Apple phones, and each phone cost over $1,000.

"I think we can get something that doesn't cost as much as our phones. Besides, Hunter's paying for it. I took one of his cards out of his wallet before I left."

"Gotcha. A burner phone it is." Jennifer turned the key, and started the car, then backed out onto the road. The two smiled as they drove toward a Walmart in search of a phone.

It was nearly noon by the time they parked across the street from a small storefront window with '**Stealth Security**' stenciled on the glass door. The office was in a strip mall, with a 7-11 on the far left, a hairdresser to the immediate right, a dry-cleaning store, a Chinese carryout, and a Verizon phone store. They were both crunching snacks, and crumbs were falling onto the seats of their mom's car. Wendy brushed her blouse off onto the floor and said, "Mom needs to clean her car."

As they laughed, they watched Steven Porowski lock the store's front door, then climb into a Honda Accord. "Showtime," Jenny screeched, and started the Equinox.

"Don't follow too close," Wendy said.

"I know, Wen, don't bother me. I can blend like a chameleon."

Wendy was quiet as they stayed three to four cars behind the Honda. Soon, they were on a four-lane highway headed out of town. Steven drove fast, pushing Jen out of her comfort zone as she tried not to gain any attention in his rearview mirror. When he took an exit, they would have been directly behind him at the stoplight. Instead of doing that, Jenny turned right, and once they got beyond the light, she made an illegal U-turn. Soon, they were a few cars behind him again. The street was lined with stores, but the retail area soon faded into a two-lane road that became a residential community.

"Do you think he's going to his home?" Wendy asked.

"Maybe." Jenny was white-knuckled, and concentrating on the rear of the Accord. It turned into a cemetery, and Jen drove past the entrance. Once beyond the graveyard entrance, she whipped the car around, and parked in front of an unknown person's house. She and Wendy both jogged to the brick curved wall on the right of the road into Slate Shore Cemetery. Luckily, the parking lot was immediately in front of them. They watched as the back of Steven's head disappeared to their right as he walked on a stone path into the rolling fields filled with headstones.

Jenny and Wendy sprinted to the far right, keeping close to a fence line sprinkled with trees of varying ages, and height. They kept an eye on the back of his head, and moved in the shadows of the trees. The grass beneath them was immaculate with no sticks, or branches to give them away, and a strong wind helped keep any noise they made, hidden. Finally, they saw Steven stop at a gravestone, and sit on a concrete bench at the end of the grave.

Jenny whipped out her phone, and attached the telescope. The scope was approximately an inch in depth. She twisted the little wheel, and whispered to Wendy. "The gravestone reads Abigail Fenton Porowski," Jennifer said.

Wendy gasped. "He talked about her at dinner. Do you think they were married?"

"It seems like it," Jenny answered, then she continued. "He's got a piece of paper in his hand, and he's reading something to his dead wife. Oh, shit, the paper got blown out of his hand, and he's chasing it across the graveyard. It's way ahead of him, and now he's given up on running after it."

"Follow it with your phone, and we'll get it after he leaves," Wendy said.

"Alright," Jenny agreed, and kept an eye on the paper as it danced across the cemetery, and stopped at a border fence. Steven spent some more time talking to his dead wife, then stood and walked back up the path to his car. The two sisters waited until he was out of sight before they skipped, slightly giddy, in the shadows of the tree line. They reached the area where the wind held the paper against a chain-link fence.

Wendy grabbed it, and read it out loud. "I got lost in your beautiful triangle -To me, it was a fountain of youth - Your waterfall - kept me strong, and tall - that's what I miss most of all, and that's the truth. Do you remember, when we were young, we fought the wolves outside our door? Then we both grew soft, and now I'm hardly hard, I've lost you forevermore."

"Well," Jenny said, "that's a little personal."

When they got back to the car, Wendy googled Abigail Fenton Porowski. "Shit, Abigail's his sister."

Chapter 4

Back at their mother's house, the two girls were filled with ideas on how to turn this stalking business around, and give Steven Porowski a taste of his own medicine. Jenny pulled up her email, and typed his first and last name without a space @gmail. Her email recognized the address as being legitimate. Then she created her email on the burner phone under AbigailFP@gmail.com, and on the subject line she wrote, "Your Poem."

Meanwhile, Wendy was looking up everything she could find about Abigail Porowski. It wasn't long before she was able to crop and copy a photo from her obituary. She also had pictures of Abigail in high school, and college. As she dug a little further into her death, she was surprised to find that the cause of her death was undetermined. She was the same age as Wendy when she died. Wendy noticed that she and Abigail shared some of the same physical features; black hair, 5'6" tall, and neither of them overweight. They both had dark eyes.

"I think this guy thought I'd be her replacement." Wendy turned her laptop around for her mom, and sister to look at the resemblance of Abigail, and Wendy.

"What a twisted bastard this guy's turning out to be," Jennifer said.

Beverly said what they were all thinking. "I think he killed her."

Wendy clutched her blouse, and leaned back in her chair, away from the laptop as if it were evil. "I had that exact thought."

Jennifer deleted "Your Poem" in the subject line, and wrote, "I'm so cold – what did you do to me, Steven?" Beneath that, in the body of the email, she wrote – "There's more to me than my body. I'm a spirit now, Steven, and I'll find you soon. I'll be a new kind of wolf at the door."

Wendy manipulated the last photo of Abigail with Photoshop. She overlapped Abigail's headshot with a skull. Then, in Paint, Wendy fogged it up, and made it look as if Abigail was melting as a live person into that of a skeleton. She designed the image to be in the text's background where Jennifer had composed the body of the email.

Their mother stepped in, and offered some advice that had a ring of wisdom to it. "Ladies, if you send that to him today, he'll know it's from you two. You need to notify Hunter as to what this man has done in regards to your son," she stated, holding Jenny's eyes as she spoke. "Let him deal with this guy, and once the dust settles, a few weeks from now, send him the email."

Wendy said, "If we're going to get Hunter involved, we should find out where this creep lives before we drop it in his lap."

"Mom," Jennifer said, "we'll need your car again, tomorrow. We'll clean it before we bring it back."

"Why does it need to be cleaned?"

"Because, mom," Wendy offered, "surveillance is a messy business."

Wendy called in sick at her job. She had yet to return to her apartment, so Jennifer followed her in her mom's car. Jen waited in the living room, peeking outside through the blinds as Wendy cleaned out her mailbox, and changed clothes before they drove to Steven's company location, and sat on the place. At one o'clock, they followed him to a restaurant. At that point, they drove away from him, and got a bite to eat on the other side of town. After they finished eating, Jennifer did what both Wendy and her mom wanted her to do yesterday. She called her husband, Hunter.

HUNTER SMITHFIELD WAS in a contemplative mood when the phone rang. He'd been thinking about his children. Was his sexual desire and fulfillment worth the destruction of a family unit? That's what had him tied up in knots. He saw his kids' future being shuffled from one parent to the next, ultimately spending most of their time with their mother. That made him think about Jennifer one day being with another man. They once had something in that department that had a depth that made it very special. Not only did they have a lengthy physical history going back to high school, but they shared the joy of having their first child, then their second, and all of the other first's; the house, the business, the luxury car, and their vacations.

Valerie had seduced him with her wit, her skin, her body, and even her smell drew him closer to her. Never having her, again, would be a life unfulfilled. It wasn't as if he was looking. Their coming together was an accident. Or was it? What does it matter? She had him, and he wanted to be had.

When he looked down at the screen, he saw Jennifer's name. He sucked in a lung full of air, and answered it. "Hey," his voice was slightly severe, and annoyed. Jennifer burst into her story.

"So, Wendy had a date with a mental guy. He followed her to her car and screamed, 'this isn't over,' or something along those lines. The next morning a notice came in her email that she got canceled from the dating site she met this guy on. It was for posting lewd photos of herself. This guy had photoshopped the image of her naked. Then Drake had that same photo pop up with Wendy naked on his tablet while he played Minecraft."

"Jesus Christ," Hunter shouted into the phone.

"I know," said Jennifer. "So, we found out where he has his office, then we followed him to a cemetery where he read his dead sister a sick poem about how he missed her body."

"How do you know what he said to his dead sister?"

"He had it on a piece of paper that the wind caught, and we pulled it off the chain-link fence where it got stuck."

"Did you call the cops?"

"No. Wendy deleted the photo, and there went our evidence. Today, we're going to sit and wait outside of his store, then follow him home to get his address. I'll give it to you as soon as I have it. Maybe you can talk to this pervert."

"Alright. How are the kids?"

"They're fine. I haven't told them that you're in love with someone that's not mommy, and that you'll be living with that person, and not us." Jennifer hit the red button, and ended the call.

Hunter shrugged as he lay his phone back on the charging station. He knew he deserved some scorn. For most of his life, this is not how he saw his future unfold. He was on the same page as Jennifer about how they viewed their life, and how it would play out. They talked about what kind of people their kids would grow into, and that one day they'd be playing with grandchildren. Now, when he thought about the future, it was more immediate. It involved rolling around in a bed with Valerie. What he got out of that was like a shot of life, a real pleasure that made him feel alive, every time. It had a spike to it with an intensity that made his anxiety disappear. The act filled him with youth; it was a rebirth. But somebody was sending pictures of Wendy, naked, to his six-year-old son, and that person needed a beat down.

Hunter wasn't a muscle-bound freak that grunted out responses to questions. But he was a muscular man that worked out as a way to network, and add to his customer base, like his golfing, and playing tennis. He was mostly a salesman, and he knew he had to maintain relationships outside of the office to grow, and being seen out and about was important. People liked it when he talked to them at the club. A friendly hello went a long way. He had a reputation of being generous, and a happy guy that was genuinely concerned about the less fortunate in the Slate Shore community.

He thought about how to deal with this freak who'd sent his boy a naked picture of his aunt. He reasoned that he'd scare the guy into walking away from his immediate, and extended family, pronto. As in, "Don't make me come back here, again."

He called Valerie into his office, and explained the whole situation. They decided that she'd come along with him, and stay in the car to make sure things were safe, and be ready if she needed to call the police. Valerie was a dark-skinned woman who was exotic to Hunter, a blonde-haired, blue-eyed man, and every time he saw her, the contrast of their skin against each other flashed before his subliminal mind. It sent a physical surge down his spine that made him slide around in his chair as if he couldn't find comfort in her presence, unless they had sex that would bring relief.

Valerie knew she made him squirm, and that tickled her on some level. She didn't like being a homewrecker. Whatever they had was so strong physically that it couldn't be denied, or shuffled off to some hidden place. They were both tired of hiding their attraction to each other. Both were old enough to make sure it wasn't a passing fancy. Ripping a family apart can't be taken lightly. Dismissing a love that they'd accidentally stumbled across would be a shame to forfeit, as well. The proximity of each other ignited a primal need.

Valerie got up, and closed the blinds on the glass door to Hunter's office. Without words, she came to his side of the desk, and wiggled out of her underwear beneath her skirt. Slowly, she leaned over the day calendar that took up most of his desk. With both hands, one on each side of her dress, she pulled the material up to her waist. Hunter shot up from his chair, and entered her from behind, holding her flanks with clenched fists, driving her hard, staring at the color difference as he slid in and out. She slowly rolled herself against him, a slight and deliberate motion that had him finish in no time. *This is living.*

JENNIFER SMILED AT Wendy, and Wendy acknowledged the little dig Jennifer made toward Hunter at the end of the phone call. They drove in silence back to a different parking space to observe Steven's office door, and parked the car. While they waited, Wendy surfed the county register's office, specifically for Steven Porowski's tax records. She found he owned a home near Madden's Inlet, not on the water, but a few blocks behind the boatyard. It was a working-class area made up of single-story houses of approximately 1000 sq. ft. McMansions, they weren't.

"I think he lives near the boatyard in a house he probably inherited from his parents," Wendy told Jennifer.

"Good to know," Jen commented. "If we lose him in traffic, we can scour the area, and find his car."

After a bit of time, and boredom, Jennifer asked Wendy, "Do you still think about Ray?"

"Too much, and too often," Wendy replied.

"Is there a formula, if you know what I mean? Like if you stop smoking cigarettes, each month without them erases a year of smoking. I don't want to be thinking about Hunter with Valerie for the next ten years."

"I know time helps, and believe it or not, you'll appreciate some of your newfound freedom. At least, for a while. You're a beautiful, intelligent woman, and I know you'll be fighting the men off in no time."

"Wen, I'm a stay-at-home mother of two small children. I don't know if I can continue to be a stay home mother, or if I need to find a job, and a place for the kids, or a nanny, or," she paused, "so many things. It's all up in the air, right now. My future, what I'd envisioned for years, doesn't exist anymore. The idea of dating at this point only attracts that part of me that wants to screw some man/boy, the age of 20, to get even with Hunter."

"I bet," said Wendy. "And I'm sure your dream boy doesn't have blonde hair, and blue eyes."

Jennifer snorted out a laugh. "No, he doesn't," she confessed. "He's got black hair, a dark complexion, maybe Hispanic, works construction, can't believe this older white lady is on top of him riding his young bod like a wild horse."

"I think you need that under your belt, Jen. The job, the money, the divorce, the visitation arrangements, the whole nine yards can take a back seat to your jumping on Pedro, and pumping his burrito until you're nothing but a soaking wet, steaming pile of refried beans."

Jennifer laughed. "It might be in his favor if he can't speak English. I'm angry at all men in general, and I might let something slip, some of that anger, and mess up my burrito ride."

"Don't mess up your burrito ride, Jen, it's important."

At four-thirty, Steven Porowski climbed into his Honda Accord, and drove out of his parking space. The two sisters pulled their moms car into traffic a few car lengths behind him, and soon recognized the route was taking them in the direction of Madden's Inlet. Less than a half-hour later, they watched Porowski enter a small ranch home, with a gravel driveway turned into mostly grass, and a shed in the back with a metal door leaning off the track. The shingles on the roof were beginning to curl. After a quick drive-by, both women felt the place was suffering from neglect. That didn't make Steven's home stand out. All the houses on the short street across from the boatyard were in disrepair.

As they drove away, Wendy said, "Those houses all look drunk."

"And depressed," Jennifer added.

Chapter 5

Hunter read the text. It had the address of the house where Steven Porowski lived. Jennifer described it as a dump. The office was closed when he and Valerie climbed into his Genesis GV80, and drove the forty minutes to the boatyard on Madden's Inlet before they turned onto the street where Porowski lived. The ride had been quiet as Hunter was mentally preparing himself for a conflict that may turn physical. He was building his anger, and feeling a surge of strength as he aggressively pulled into the gravel and grass driveway.

After slamming the car door shut, he marched to the front of Steven's house, and knocked on the wooden frame, causing a small pile of flaking paint to collect at his feet. He looked around, and caught a quick glimpse of himself in the glass of the aluminum storm door. He listened intently, and thought he heard a shuffling sound from inside the house. Then the door opened about a third of the way, and Steven stared at Hunter. They were both approximately the same height. Steven said, "Yes?" as he held Hunter's angry gaze with curiosity.

Hunter stepped over the threshold in one smooth movement, and with his palms up, and his fingers out, he pushed Steven backward, and yelled at the same time, "You sent naked pictures to my six-year-old son, you sick fuck!"

Steven stumbled backward, and as he did, he tripped on his own feet, and landed cockeyed on his right side. His eyes grew large, and he made no move to stand. At that same instant, Hunter noticed a slight odor of garbage. He was in a hall that should have been open to the living room. There were boxes, bags, newspapers and magazines stacked from the floor to the ceiling. Steven was an apparent hoarder. Hunter stared at him, crumpled into a pile on the dingy floor. Hunter said, "Look at you, dude, you're a hoarder, you're alone, you're sending pictures to a six-year-old, and that could get you time in prison. You should schedule some couch time with someone, and stop this destructive behavior." Hunter glanced around, and he couldn't help but have a wave of pity. "You make me come back, again," he pointed his index finger, "I'm going to kill your ass."

In the car, it took Hunter driving to the interstate to come down from the mountain of testosterone he'd climbed to confront Steven. When he spoke, it was a short yell as if he had to release the words, or he'd explode. "He's a hoarder; his house stunk. What the hell's the matter with a guy like that?"

Valerie said, "Hoarding is the result of some kind of traumatic loss."

Hunter merged onto the highway, and glanced at Valerie. She continued, "Like the death of a parent, or a divorce, something like that."

"Who gives a shit," Hunter said. "If he sends another email to Drake, I'll be on him like stink on shit."

Valerie shifted her posture as a kind of involuntary displeasure with the way Hunter was acting. Her attraction for him was partly due to his being level-headed, and composed under pressure. This side of him wasn't exactly a red flag; it was just something she'd file away as one of his extremes, like his need to have sex twice a day.

"Hoarders are locked into a mental state of not wanting to lose anything else," she stated.

Hunter was concentrating on driving, and calmly said, "I told him he needed help. I smelled garbage, and saw all this trash piled to the ceiling. He was lying on the floor, and it made me feel sorry for him. If he sends any more emails, I'll be back with the police."

Over the following weeks, Hunter and Valerie moved in together in a rented townhome near the office. Valerie's mother had given her a hard time. She knew Hunter had a family, and her daughter had destroyed it. Valerie pleaded her case. "It happened organically, Mom. I didn't set out to hurt anyone; I was only there to work. Something outside of my control developed, and I couldn't dismiss my feelings, and shake all these urges. Finally, we both acted on what was building; this tension that we couldn't fight. It was such a strong attraction; love, mixed with desire, and passion."

"Mm-hum, you pushed past the fence line to get into the weeds, child, and all this race mixing ain't nothing but planting flowers around the outhouse. You'll see; people in Slate Shore don't most of them embrace mixed couples."

"I know, Momma, but we're not children. We're strong enough to stand with each other, no matter what."

Jennifer had asked Hunter for an allowance, and child support until she could set up someone to watch the kids after school, and find a job. It was heart-wrenching for her to think about Hunter with another woman. She had a mental vision of him lost in the excitement of having a different body to look at, and talk to, someone with a new personality. All that newness must be a real turn on to him. It made her think she'd become some kind of fixture; one he'd grown tired of seeing. She wondered if he'd resented her, and if so, for how long?

The children were her first concern, and she'd told Hunter that they both needed to give the kids some extra attention during this period of adjustment. He'd agreed, so Jennifer took Olivia and Drake along with Wendy to Happy Land, and let the kids eat whatever they wanted, and go on every ride. While they were on a child's ride, the two sisters talked. Wendy asked, "How's the job search coming?"

Jennifer answered, "I'm not looking for work, right now. I'll stay home until he's out of guilt, and starts pressuring me to make some money. And," she said with a slight smirk, "there's a new club that just opened downtown. It's getting great reviews. I thought the two of us could get dressed up, a bit skanky-sluttish, then I can leave with someone, and you can go to my house, and relieve the babysitter. Don't tell the kids Mommy's getting busy with a young athlete, or that she'll be working out all night, and won't be home until she can hardly walk."

Saturday evening found the two women dressed provocatively, and managing to walk in high heels. Wendy was strolling in a pair of pewter-colored, waltz-backed, beaded strappy four-inch heels with a silver skirt that barely covered her underwear. She had a silk blouse to match. Jennifer managed to stand upright in bright red Flamenco heels with white straps, and toes painted to match. Both chose shimmering cloth that left little to the imagination from the cleavage reveal. At a glance, the two could be high-end escorts.

In the car, Wendy's car, since she was planning on returning alone, Jennifer commented, "We look like Vegas streetwalkers."

"What's your point?" Wendy joked, and they both cracked up.

The traffic was light, and soon they were walking down a set of five steps to a single door with an illuminated overhang that had the words **French-Underground** written in cursive fluorescent tubing. Through the door they could hear the massive thump of a bass beat. A huge man opened the door after a knock from Wendy, and the bouncer smiled once he saw the two women on the other side. "Welcome to the French Underground. Don't cause too much trouble, okay, ladies?"

Wendy said, "I'll be good. I can't answer for her," she smirked as she tilted her head toward Jennifer.

Jennifer said, "I'll try and restrain myself."

"You do that," the large doorman said, leaning in close enough to smell Jennifer's perfume. "I'd hate to have to grab you around your waist, and manhandle you out of here," he smiled, once again, with a bright set of white teeth.

Jennifer said, "Ah, what time do you get off?"

The handsome, black man, answered, "Wouldn't you like to know?"

Jennifer took that as, we're just playing around, I'm not getting serious. She smiled, and once inside, she had to practically scream into Wendy's ear over top of the techno music. "I can't even throw myself at a man."

"He had a ring on, Jen; it was the size of a hula hoop. The guys a mountain."

"Oh, I didn't notice the ring."

"Now that you're single, you need to look at that."

The dance floor was not yet full since nine p.m. was considered early. Laser lights shone on the ceiling, the tables, and the walls. The sisters ordered white wine, then suddenly, Jennifer's face turned into a collapsed mess. She had mascara running down over her cheeks as she turned to Wendy. "I don't want to be here. On Saturday nights, we'd cuddle, and watch a movie." She dug in her purse, and pulled out a cloth to wipe her face.

Wendy reached her hand out, and held onto Jennifer's hand. "I know it's not the same, no kids, I wasn't married, but we did live together. When I came home to an empty house, and read Ray's note, "I'm just a check in a box,' I was devastated. It took me a long time to realize I'd taken our relationship for granted, and that's what he was saying with the checking off a box. Suddenly, I had to make the rent payment by myself, and start dating again. And you see how that turned out; a pyscho is stalking me."

Jennifer smiled, and said, "You sure know how to cheer a girl up." She pulled out her pocket mirror, and excused herself to go freshen up in the lady's room.

Wendy pulled out her phone, and checked her email. As she scrolled down, erasing advertisements, she came across an email; stevenporowski at gmail.com. Under subject, it read – Whore! – and in the body, Steven wrote – "You and your sister are both dressed like prostitutes."

When Jennifer came back to the table, Wendy turned her phone around to show her sister the email. Jennifer said, "What am I supposed to be looking for?"

Wendy turned the phone back to view the screen, and look at the email. It was gone.

Chapter 6

Over the next few hours, having left the club soon after the email, they researched disappearing emails in Jennifer's home. Several apps advertised magic text. Text that would disappear like invisible ink, and accepted by a variety of servers. "This is maddening. We have no evidence," Wendy said, tossing down her phone on a couch cushion.

"I'll be right back," Jennifer said. "I'm going to get my burner phone, and send him an email from his dead sister."

AbigailFP@gmail.com. Subject, "Your Sick Poem." In the body – "I'm so cold, Stevie, why did you do this to me? I did everything you asked. I even told you I loved you so that you wouldn't kill me. But you always wanted more; my body, my mind, and finally, my soul."

If they weren't buzzed on booze, and were sober during the light of day, the sisters would have pushed it through one of the disappearing apps they read online. However, they were nearly sloppy drunk, drowning in self-pity, and at two in the morning, their thinking was swelled with false bravado, and were slightly squirmy in the logic department. They treated the email as if it were a punch to Steven's face. The phone was cussed at, and flipped off with the middle finger in their slurry interpretation of what they had just done. They put the proverbial nail in the coffin; it was only in the morning, after several cups of coffee, that the thought of poking an angry stalker that reads sexually provocative poems to his dead sister might not have been the wisest of choices.

Their mother, Beverly, was perturbed that Jennifer had hired a baby sitter, and not let her watch the kids. Jennifer didn't have the heart to tell her that Drake was in love with the babysitter, and wanted the cute 13-year-old, Tiffany Lanklin, to watch them. Wendy asked Jen where six-year-old Drake's wedding would be held, to which Jennifer replied, "I guess Dinosaur Land."

"We shouldn't have sent that email. It's like stirring up a wasp nest," Wendy said.

"Oh, God," Jen said as she rubbed her forehead. "Why did we do it?"

"Bad genes, environmental pollution, and too much wine," Wendy offered.

Their action hung in the air like a curse. How could it be removed? They couldn't exactly send their stalker a bouquet of roses, and have their little joke be forgiven. That's especially true after Hunter had knocked him to the floor, and warned him. They decided to text Hunter, and tell him that Steven was still stalking them, watched them on Saturday night, and sent a horrible email that disappeared after being read.

Hunter, with Valerie, drove back to Steven's home several times. His car was there, but no one answered the door, and Hunter couldn't hear anyone inside the house. He even went to Steven's office in the strip mall. It was always closed, and dark inside. Hunter wondered if the guy had packed up, and left town. On the stoop of the house they had bought to raise their children, he told Jennifer when he came to pick up the kids for the weekend; he couldn't find Steven, anywhere. He assumed Steven had left town. Three weeks had passed since the last Steven incident. They'd all hoped that Steven had moved away, and that all the drama was over and done.

Sunday morning, in his pajamas making pancakes, and goofing around with the children in their rented townhome, a knock came on the door. When Hunter opened it, two detectives showed their badges.

Behind them, standing at the base of the door landing, were several policemen. The detectives showed Hunter a search warrant for his premises, including his office, and car. The other detective showed Hunter the warrant for his arrest. Hunter asked if he could take a minute, and read the warrant of arrest. The detective said, yes.

The magistrate signed the complaint. The reason for his arrest was probable cause in a crime. The crime committed involved the disappearance of Steven Porowski. The detective standing over Hunter as he sat in a chair in the living room reading the document, said, "We ran this past the prosecuting attorney, and the judge who issued the arrest." Hunter read his full name, and the address of the townhome he rented with Valerie. Everything was correct, and it all slammed into him like a sledgehammer. He was stunned.

The children started crying. Valerie did everything she could to calm them down. Hunter gave the detectives the key, and the security code for his office. The cops let him call his attorney, and change out of his pajamas. Valerie explained everything to Jennifer when she returned the children earlier than expected on Sunday. Jennifer used the card that Valerie gave her to call Detective McDermott. She requested a meeting, along with her sister, as soon as possible.

Beverly came to Jennifer's house to watch Olivia and Drake. Wendy and Jen drove in Wendy's car to the Slate Shore Police Department on Sandridge Road, across the street from the new Walmart, and Perkins Barbeque. The desk sergeant asked them to have a seat before he buzzed Detective McDermott on his phone. He informed him that Jennifer Smithfield, and Wendy Valise, were in the lobby.

A six-foot-something man, who looked like he knew his way around a bench press, came around the corner by the elevators with his shiny shoes echoing off the terrazzo floor. He had a military buzz cut that revealed a salt and pepper color scheme, which appeared a little premature for a man whose facial age looked to be in his early forties at the most. He introduced himself. "I'm sorry to be meeting you both under these circumstances. I'm Detective McDermott from the homicide division. I understand you two have some information that you felt was relevant to this case."

Wendy and Jen looked at each other. Both were taken aback that the detective didn't guide them into a conference room. They simultaneously thought what they had to say wasn't being taken seriously. "Is there somewhere you want us to go to take our statements outside of this public waiting area?" Jennifer asked.

Detective McDermott looked around at the empty lobby, then back at Jen. "There's nobody here except us girls."

Wendy and Jennifer both leaped to a quick assumption that the handsome man was some macho asshole. "Look," Wendy began, "I started a correspondence with this guy Steven Porowski on a dating site called City Singles. We met at the Iron Horse Restaurant, and during our conversation, he started making me feel uncomfortable. I told him I was leaving, and asked him not to follow me to my car, or email me again. When I climbed inside my car, he grabbed the door, flung it open, and yelled at me that this wasn't over, and I hadn't heard the last of him. Then, later on that evening, I got a notice from City Singles that I'd posted inappropriate material, and the message showed me naked on a couch. It was photoshopped because I wasn't," she shook her head. "It wasn't me, okay? The next morning, Drake, my nephew, who is six-years-old, had the same picture show up on his tablet when he was playing Minecraft."

"Did you notify the police?"

"No, I didn't, because in my haste, I deleted the picture, then I instantly regretted it. I don't think it would have made any difference because this guy sends emails out that evaporate, or whatever the term is for disappearing emails. We looked it up. It's a thing." Wendy took a breath. "We followed him from his job to a cemetery where he read a sick poem to his dead sister. The wind caught it, and blew it out of his hands. We found it stuck to a fence. At first, we thought it was to his wife, but it was his sister. Later, we followed him from his job to his home. We told Hunter about it, and he went to Steven's house, and warned him off.

"But that didn't work. Jen and I," she pointed to Jen, "Hunter's wife, but they're separated, went on a night out. He sent me an email calling us whore's for how we dressed when we went out. The email vanished almost as soon as I read it. He's a devious techno Geek, and you won't find a body because it doesn't exist. He's still alive. He's an intelligent, sick dude. I think he killed his sister. That's because her death was unknown." Wendy stopped talking as if she could now rest, having presented her argument before the court.

"That's an interesting story," Detective McDermott folded his arms over his chest as he stood over both women sitting in chairs. "But we have Hunter Smithfield on tape inside Steven's home telling him he's going to kill him. Then we have this massive pool of blood; too much for someone to have spilled, then survive. The blood belongs to Steven Porowski; we checked the DNA on his toothbrush, and empty soda bottles in the trash. And we have his laptop with a suspicious email to him, from an unknown. I suppose you don't know anything about that?" Detective McDermott glanced from Wendy to Jennifer. "It's from his dead sister."

Wendy and Jennifer turned pale. "Listen," Mc Dermott continued. "Saying that someone killed his sister because you had a bad dinner date is slanderous, and you have no evidence. If it's because he smelled funny, or his eyes were too close together, that's not the kind of thing that holds up in court. So, bring me some evidence about these disappearing emails; otherwise, it's all hearsay."

In the car, Wendy said to Jennifer, "For the record, he smelled kind of nice. But his eyes were a little too close together, so he probably killed her."

"Ha, ha," Jennifer said with tight lips. "This is serious. We need to get a techno-geek who can figure out how to retrieve disappearing emails, and show that smug detective what we're talking about."

HUNTER CALLED A LAWYER; a guy he'd known since he was five. Winston Markham was a contract specialist, and his clients were large construction companies that built neighborhoods, and apartment complexes. He represented the insurance companies that the builders used for liability coverage. Winston spent his days taking photos of stucco, and backhoe's digging up sewer lines. His courtroom experience was also lacking because his cases ended in mediation. That background was a far cry from what Hunter needed, which was an experienced criminal law attorney. However, when a crisis happens, a person needs to start somewhere.

Hunter had Winston's number in his phone. The two were often golfing partners at the club. "Hey, buddy," Winston answered on the second ring.

"Man, I'm glad you answered, Winston. I'm in jail, and charged with murdering Steve Porowski."

"Who's Steve Porowski?"

"A guy that was sending naked photos to my six-year-old."

"Shit, Hunter. I thought you were going to hit me with the punch line when I asked who's Steve Porowski."

"No," Hunter sagged at the desk where he was seated at a bolted-down table. "I wish it were a joke. It's a nightmare, and I need your help pronto, man."

"Are you at the Slate Shore Police Department?"

"Yes, I'm in a holding cell. The cops plan on transferring me to the city jail in a couple of hours."

"I'll call a bail bondsman I know, and I'll be there within an hour."

"Thanks, dude."

Hunter had chewed his fingernails to the meat. He hated himself for falling apart. Being charged with murder can do that to a person. Valerie was at their townhome frantically marching back and forth from the living room to the kitchen, all while talking on the phone to her cousin, Melvin, who was supposed to be a computer wizard. A knock came from the door, and Valerie told Melvin she'd call him back in about twenty minutes.

When she opened the door, Steve Porowski viciously stuck a syringe full of sodium pentothal into Valerie's chest as he pushed her backward. She fell on the carpet, almost hitting her head on a bookstand. "What the f...," was all she said as she slipped immediately into unconsciousness. Steven walked to the back door, where an alley ran behind the townhomes. He focused his gaze on a big green trashcan with wheels that the county provided to every resident. Steven pulled a hoody over his head, adjusted his gloves, walked across the lawn, and grabbed the trashcan handle. He pulled the plastic container up the four steps, and into the home.

Not being strong enough to pick Valerie up, he tilted the can on its side, and pushed her into the empty cavity. He then struggled to raise the can back up. He ended up leaning a dining room chair on the floor, with the back of it under the trashcan. With the chair's leverage, he raised the can a few inches, and slid two books under it. Slowly, methodically, Steven raised the can enough to be upright. He used the wheels to haul Valerie across the living room carpet, and returned to the back door. Straining, he was able to hang on as he lowered the can down the steps.

It took him almost a half hour to drag-pull the plastic trash container to the back gate on the privacy fence. He slipped around to the front yard using a side gate, and walked a block and a half to his work van. There were no more magnetic signs on the van's body advertising his business. The white work van was as plain as a sponge cake. He drove it to the gate in their backyard. The gate swung inward, and he hauled the trashcan to the side of the van. He slid a ramp out that he used for delivering servers, and installation supplies. He was able to pull the can into the truck, and close the gate. It was nearly dark when he drove away with Valerie. In another two hours, he'd leave the eastern shore of Maryland, and be moving towards Virginia's mountains.

Chapter 7

Peach Hill is a 1600-foot-tall, round-topped mountain in the foothills of the Blue Ridge mountain range. On the southeastern side of the hill is a developed community of middle-class ranch homes on five-acre lots. Some of the lands have been tilled, and terraced into farmable property. Other sections have not undergone manipulation, and are kept manicured by various goats; brown Nubians, going back to Africa, and white Alpine goats that have DNA linked to the Netherlands. Both varieties give somewhere from a half-gallon, to three quarters of milk, a day.

The road to the top of this rocky land had sharp angles, stunted locust, and walnut trees, a series of switchbacks, and if it's winter, this is as far as you want to drive. The northern face remains in shadows. Rain becomes ice, and the road becomes treacherous. Steven Porowski has his van parked outside of a cabin with electricity, and running water, on the dark side of the mountain, but there's no septic system for waste. The kitchen drain dumps onto the surface of the leaf-filled hill. A leaning outhouse stands some 30 feet behind the cabin.

Steven waited until Valerie awoke in the van. When she did, still groggy, he marched her with a rifle in her side to a bed where he tied her up with electrical wire fished through Styrofoam pipe insulation, to avoid ligature marks. He had a big jug of water with a bent plastic straw for her to suck on anytime she became thirsty. Above the bed, near her right arm, was a plastic bag filled with a yellow substance. A tube dangled loosely beneath it, and would soon be dripping into her cardiovascular system. He had it set up to feed into a vein under her armpit. The veins are deep in that area. A group of nerves travel under the arm to serve the wrist, and fingers. It'll take him a while to find what he's looking for, and cause some discomfort with the long thin needle, but rest assured, he'll find the vein, and adjust the drip.

HUNTER AND WINSTON Markham both searched the townhome for Valerie. Her phone was on the living room floor, and her car was out front. Hunter discovered the large trashcan was missing, and he noticed impressions in the ground from the bottom of the steps to the back gate. There were also green plastic bits on the toe edge of each step. A story was unfolding before his eyes, and he couldn't believe what he was seeing. "Why?" he asked as his eyes filled with horror, and mist. "Why is this happening? This shit makes no sense," he declared, staring at Winston, who seemed as baffled as anyone.

"You need to call the cops straight away, buddy."

As Hunter pressed 911, his mind raced with a burning question; why? Valerie had nothing to do with him threatening Porowski. This pyscho Steven was going after everyone except Wendy, and she was the one who instigated his rage in the first place. Nothing was linear. His mathematical accountant mind was having a hard time putting pieces of this puzzle in place. A thought crossed his mind. He had an audit with the IRS on behalf of a client this week. How could he possibly represent the client with anything close to professionalism?

After calling the emergency number, he spoke to his head accountant, and put him in charge of everything. He gave a brief explanation, and ended the call. He called Jennifer, and explained the situation. He begged her to send her mom and the kids somewhere safe. He lowered his voice and said, "Jen, I know I don't deserve it, but I need your help. I'm in trouble, and it all has to do with this guy Porowski. I can't even think about what he's doing to Valerie. You've got to help me find her, and get those ghost emails printed out, and linked to this guy. I feel Valerie's disappearance will be the next charge against me. I'm out on bail, and have Winston Markham as my temporary lawyer until we can find an excellent criminal lawyer. Call him with any progress. I've got to go." Before disconnecting on his phone, Hunter asked, "Can I count on you?"

Jennifer took in a deep breath and said, "Yes, I'll do all I can."

Wendy couldn't believe the shit storm that was unfolding around her.

VALERIE, HER HEAD CLEARING after being marched into the cabin, asked Porowski, "Why are you doing this to me, Steven?" Her black eyes were widening in mad fear as she got a glimpse of the water bottle with a straw, her bound wrists, and tied ankles. "I've done nothing to you," she added, her voice rising in near hysterics.

Steven admired his work as he surveyed the bed, and his victim. "Let me tell you a story, lady. My father was a mean drunk, and a stupid thief. You see that bottle of yellow liquid? That's EDTA; a substance used for chelation; the removal of metals from your blood. For instance, lead poisoning, or mercury poisoning, and for people who experience an iron overdose from eating certain kinds of seafood, like shrimp. Back in the '90s, there were chelation treatment centers all over the states. They were used as a cure-all for people too damaged, and old, for heart surgery, and folks with high cholesterol, and elevated blood pressure. It was snake oil, and the medical association eventually shut it down. My father, the genius, broke into a clinic, and stole cases of the EDTA solution. Along with the hoses, valves, and so on to administer the solution. He thought people would come to our house, and pay for him to give them the treatment. Nobody came, and the supplies eventually gathered dust in our basement. Dad went to prison for robbing, and killing a man at a rest area. In prison, somebody stabbed him, and he died. Meanwhile, I was twelve when I began taking care of Abigail, my sister, and the two of us watched our mother drink herself to death. I loved Abigail, not just as a sister, but as a friend, and a lover, and we became inseparable. But then," Steven's voice began to become tight, and hesitant, his hands became animated, and his face turned into a sneer, "someone like you came along — someone who didn't respect the sanctity and bond of an existing relationship. And my sister, the love of my life, wanted to move out, and live with this," he was spitting as he began to scream, and Valerie moved her head back as much as she could from the repulsion, "animal named Mathew D'Angelo. And do you know what I did, miss home wrecker? I strapped her to the same bed that you're in, and I gave her so much chelation, she died. Then I placed her body in her car in a fast-food parking lot. The coroner told me he thought she had severe anemia, but he couldn't confirm it. And you wouldn't believe what I did a year later to Mathew D'Angelo. Oh, he's spread out all over this mountain," he waved his arm in a great arc. "What a wimp," he laughed, his voice dropping an octave as he began to calm down. "He cried like a little bitch. So, I think you can guess what's going to happen to you, and why. You and your boss have been screwing like rabbits, with no concern about the impact on his children. All you care about is your selfish needs. And now you'll pay. The hair under your arm will hide the needle mark. It's small, anyway. And your cause of death, in a different state, with a different coroner, will be undetermined, just like Abigail," Steven smiled as he stared at Valerie.

He never used my name. He's dehumanized me, and I need to make him see me. Valerie was doing her best to assess the situation. "It happened by accident, Steven, by proximity. We didn't set out to hurt anyone. But we fell in love, and once we did, we couldn't stand to be apart from each other. Can't you understand that it was love, a love so strong that we had to be together?"

"Enough! Shut up!" He ran his hand through his dark, greasy hair. One of his legs started jumping on his six-foot, thin, wiry frame. He leaped to her side, and forcefully grabbed her face with his soft hand, squeezing her cheeks until she wanted to cry. His breath smelled like old eggs. "One more word, and I'll get the iron. You ask Mathew D'Angelo how that feels," his spit, with bits of an Egg McMuffin, were landing on her face. She closed her eyes. "When you see him in hell!" With that, Porowski let go. Her face was stinging from his grip. *Don't piss him off; he's volatile, and crazy.*

As suddenly as he turned violent, Steven returned to calm. His rage, mysteriously, perhaps chemically, placated as he strolled, and hummed over to the metal sink with a built-in drainboard. It was a combination unit with two drawers; one to each side of the sink, and four doors underneath. The ceramic coating on the unit was chipped, and the chrome handles were pitted with rust. He turned on the faucet, and filled a plastic container with water. Then he turned toward Valerie, who was watching him with disbelief. She knew, on the one hand, this was happening, but if she closed her eyes, and went deep enough, maybe she could go somewhere else until this was all over. Hunter must be frantic, and looking for her. Was he even out of jail? It was all too much, and a tear slid down her cheek.

"I'm pouring the water through this filter that will remove all the metal. This way, when you drink it, you won't be replenishing any metal once the chelation begins taking it out of your system. If you don't have enough copper, zinc, iron, and nickel in your body, your respiratory system shuts down." He had his back to her. She watched his elbows move in front of him before he turned around, and smiled at her. "I know what you're thinking. Will it hurt? The chelation will feel warm in your body as it spreads. You'll drift away," he smiled as if the news he'd given her was all excellent. Congratulations, you've won first prize, and guess what? It's death.

Chapter 8

Beverly looked at her two daughters and said, "I'd like to make a suggestion." Both girls turned toward their mother. Once she had their full attention, she said, "Go to one of those ancestry sites, and look up Steven's family tree. See if he had uncles, or aunts where he might have inherited their property. Check out the counties they lived in, and see if Porowski has some land, or something, near their property. He went somewhere, and he doesn't impress me as a world traveler."

Jenifer glanced at Wendy. Wendy nodded, and Jenifer turned to her mom. "Brilliant, mom, I'm on it. Meanwhile, keep looking for a forensic technician."

The internet has all the answers you need if you know how to coax it out of the ethereal clouds of technology. After several phone calls, and a little pleading, Marshal Thomas in Washington D.C., some two hours' drive away, said he would come out to look at their devices, and see what he could find. He was an expert at reverse engineering. In his recent past, Marshal had worked for a central bank in their fraud department. After the bank, he worked for an insurance company in their trace attributions center. Marshal now worked for himself, and believed there would be no problem recovering deleted, or encrypted, information. His charge was $2,500 a day, and he assured the women it wouldn't be more than two days.

"He sounded black," Jennifer blurted out after they disconnected the phone call, which was on speaker.

"Yes," Beverly said. "Why, dear?"

Wendy chimed in, and explained it all to her mom. "Jen couldn't close the deal, and hop on a brown pole when we went out the other night, mom. Instead, she had a breakdown, and then we found out that we were sick-stalked. So, who knows, maybe Marshal Thomas will be a hunk, and Jennifer can have a little get even sex."

Beverly's mouth dropped like a tailgate on an F150 Ford pickup in a parking lot party at a NASCAR race. Jennifer patted her mom's arm. "It's a different time, mom. I need to get even with Hunter."

"And," Wendy said, "maybe our Jen can work in a little discount."

Beverly didn't know if they were pulling her leg, or not. She returned to concentrate on the ancestry search form, and realized they needed more information than a first, and last name. They checked the county records, and found Steven's full name from the house deed. His middle name was Marcel. They also had his parents' names, but not his mother's maiden name. With only his parents' names, they were still limited. They needed to have his mother's maiden name to help the system take a deep dive.

Wendy called her boss, and briefly explained what was going on with her family. Her boss couldn't believe what she was hearing, and gave Wendy an extended amount of time off with one week's worth of her sick leave. The plan was to have her go to the courthouse in the morning, and search for the parents' birth certificates, and marriage application. She would take her mother's phone with her, and leave hers for Marshal to check out the disappearing emails she'd read.

The following morning, Wendy went to the courthouse looking for a marriage certificate for Steven's parents. It was a long shot. Who knows in what county, or state, they were married? The woman behind the counter was accommodating, and in no time, Wendy had what she wanted. She snapped a couple of photos with her moms' phone, and sent the long-ago newlyweds' names to Jennifer. By the time she arrived back at her moms' house, the order from the ancestry tracing site had come back for Steven Marcel Porowski. It arrived in a PDF file on Jennifer's laptop. With a pencil, and paper poised, Beverly and Jennifer bent over the screen, and took notes. They found the name of two uncles on his father's side who had lived in the area. His mother's relatives were on the west coast, a far cry from Maryland's eastern shore.

As they jotted down the information, they realized one of the uncles had a family, and he most likely passed on his property in Baltimore to his children. The other uncle lived in a small town across the Potomac River in Colonial Beach, Virginia. It was approximately an hour's drive from where they were in Slate Shore. In this case, Wendy was sent to go to the courthouse in Westmorland County, Virginia, and find out what happened to the property.

Two hours later, Wendy was scanning through microfilm. She had the information on a date when the uncle had died. Her search began in the year before his death, and it wasn't long before she discovered the uncle's property had sold at an auction two years after he died. "Shit," she mumbled, causing a woman behind the nearby desk to give her a librarian's stare. Disheartened, Wendy drove back over the 301 bridge toward her mother's home.

HUNTER WAS TEETERING, approaching a break down on the living room couch. His head was too heavy for his neck, and his legs were spread apart, and anchored to the floor. Each leg had an elbow nailed to it just above the knee. His view of the carpet, with an open hand on each temple, didn't register. His thoughts were swimming in mud, and he felt like he'd fallen through a rabbit hole. The question of why circled back until he realized asking it was wasting time. He needed to find Valerie. The visions he had of her, and what was, or could be happening to her, tormented him. He raised his head, and met the eyes of Detective McDermott. "What are you doing to find her?" It came out louder than he'd planned. McDermott didn't like Hunter, and it showed.

"I don't know what's going on here. What I can say is that two people linked to you have gone missing. That leaves a bad taste in my mouth, and I'm not sure you should be out on bail."

Winston Markham, the lawyer, turned toward the detective. "The bail was set, then satisfied. So, let's stop wasting time talking about the bail. Valerie Washington is missing. Her phone was lying on the floor. It looks like something pretty heavy was dragged in the trashcan to the back alley. Scrape marks are on the back steps; it looks like the trash can was tilted, and fragments are on the stairs. I came here with Mr. Smithfield, and he was shocked, and you're talking about bail. For God's sake, man, do your job; canvas the area for witnesses. This kidnapping was the work of that sick bastard, Porowski. Find him, and you'll realize my client is innocent."

In the back of McDermott's mind was something he was keeping to himself. Porowski's work van was AWOL, and that jiggled a bit in the gray matter of the detective's brain. Hunter was snow-white, and he seemed genuinely distraught. The detective did a quick sweep of the room. Not much had changed since they'd had their search. The forensic team were on their way. He doubted they'd find anything of significance. If Porowski was behind all these events, he most likely wore gloves, and made sure there were no witnesses.

"Why would Porowski take Valerie?" McDermott asked Hunter.

Hunter checked himself. He was about to yell out, 'How the hell would I know?', but that would further push the detective away, and he needed him. "Maybe," he spoke with hesitation, "maybe he's getting even with me for yelling at him, and pushing him to the floor. Why he isn't going after Wendy, the origin of his anger, is beyond me. I left him crumpled on the floor in a house with a slight hint of garbage, and obviously, he had hoarding issues. I felt sorry for the guy, and I told him to look around. He's alone, he's a hoarder, and he should seek out some professional help. Maybe that sent him over the edge. I don't understand the man. I keep circling back to Wendy; she's the one that started all this, and nothing has happened to her except for being ejected from a dating site. Valerie was in the car, waiting for me, and I don't think Steven even saw her. She's a sweetheart, and told me that hoarders are hanging onto everything they can as a way to keep from losing any more. She explained that the hoarding starts from a divorce, or a death. Even an empty nest can trigger the need to cling to stuff. It's like Valerie was trying to get me to see Steven's mental illness, and beyond the tall, skinny guy that sent my kid a naked, and doctored, photo. I don't know what set him off. At this point, I couldn't care less. I want to find Valerie before he does something to her."

McDermott felt a pang of sorrow for Hunter. Not much, but his pain was palpable enough to hang your hat on. The guy was suffering, and that was becoming obvious. The detective nodded, and walked to his unmarked Ford Interceptor. He called in an all-points bulletin on the white work van that was missing.

Chapter 9

Her muscles were screaming, and she'd soiled her pants. Sleep came in the shape of awful dreams. Her cousin, Cricket, known for jumping from item to item, escaped from juvenile detention when he was 15. The circumstances were different, but the result was the same goal. She closed her eyes, and concentrated on looking at the situation. Anew, she stared at her wrist. A yellow wire was threaded through Styrofoam pipe insulation, and wrapped around her wrist. It was twisted, and extremely tight. The end of the wire was bare copper from inside the yellow sheathing. That wire was twisted around itself, and shaped into a small circle. Another piece of the yellow cable passed through that circle, and fastened to the bedpost.

If she pushed her arm toward the bedpost, the wire would make an arc four inches tall, and when she dropped her arm, it pulled tight, once again. If she did that enough times, and quickly, would it be enough to heat the wire, and break? Next, she moved to her legs, which had the same setup. She couldn't reach the wire with her teeth. And the needle in her arm hurt when she moved around. Should she accept her fate, and make peace with whatever higher power is out there? A God with a hands-off kind of ruling technique. Was he observing her, now?

Where was Steven? She raised her head as high as she could. The cabin was dark, and quiet. She'd heard of women lifting cars to save their child. Could she create a surge of strength enough to rip the bedpost from the frame? She pulled with her left hand, the weaker of the two, but the one that didn't have a needle taped to her armpit. She pulled, and strained. Nothing moved, or changed, or even creaked.

Valerie fell back asleep, and dreamed. She woke with a start after hearing someone say, "Break your wrist." She attributed that voice to her thinking about escaping before she closed her eyes. She stared at her left hand, and wiggled her fingers. She pulled without her full strength to get a gauge on how small she'd need to make her hand to fit through the wire. A thought floated to the surface. She could fill her mouth with water from the straw, and spit it on her hand, over, and over if that's what it takes to lubricate her skin before giving it everything. *If he catches you, he'll use the iron.*

THEY PRINTED THE MATERIAL that came from the ancestral web site. There were passport photos, birth documents, and a newspaper article with a picture of a 13-year-old Steven standing beside his uncle with one foot on top of a six-point buck. The story explained that Steven Porowski was hunting on his uncle's property when he saw the deer. The uncle was very proud of his nephew. It was the first deer registered in Burlington County on the opening day of deer season.

Porowski's report was neatly stacked, then set aside. The neglect was because Marshal Thomas was at the front door, and that was their immediate concern. Marshal, used to pinpointing a phishing scheme, malicious software, Malware, and denial of service blackmailing crimes, thought this assignment would be a slam dunk. He had with him a two-wheeled dolly with metallic suitcases strapped to the frame. He wore an opened cardigan sweater. The weather was turning cold in late October, and there was a chill in the air.

Thomas stood inside the living room, and immediately removed his sweater. The temperature inside the home was sweltering. He glanced at Jennifer as he unpacked his equipment. He had a bit of a pleading stare, and Jennifer said, "My mother has a glandular condition, so she keeps the house warm." He nodded, after first lingering on Jennifer's large eyes. In return, Jennifer did not hide her assessment of Marshal. She looked him up and down, and smiled. He glanced down from his six-foot-two stance, and returned her smile with equal pleasure. Then, Marshal pulled his shoulders back, stuck out his big hand to Beverly, and introduced himself.

"Hi, Mrs. Valise, I'm Marshal Thomas. I'm sorry to be meeting you under challenging circumstances. I'll do my best to find out who sent these ghost emails, and retrieve them."

"Please call me Beverly. This is my daughter, Jennifer."

Marshal smiled with the whitest teeth she thinks she'd ever seen. They were perfect, and when he shook Jennifer's hand, a maroon plum blossomed under his cheeks. They looked at each other like two sex-starved teenagers planning to meet under the bleachers on the visitor's side. With a physical tension in the air, Marshal had to push past his attraction. He finished unpacking, and asked where he could set up his computers.

Beverly guided Marshal to the dining room table. The kids were shooed out, and told to go to the kitchen table. Marshal said, "Cute kids."

Jennifer said, "Yes, they are."

Marshal adjusted two large screens on the laptops. Out of a pouch inside one of the two cases, he inserted a zip drive. He turned from Beverly, to Jennifer. "This takes a little while. I'm installing an intrusion detective device." While the program ran on one of his laptops, he plugged an Amphenol cord into Wendy's phone. "This should soon give me an electronic footprint, which will show me how he entered her email."

Soon, Marshal was staring at a list of graphs, and numbers. He began mumbling to himself as his fingers danced across the keyboard like Elton John. "Interesting," he scratched his chin.

"What's interesting," Jennifer asked staring at the screen, which might as well have been a Chinese poem to an ancient Emperor. "He used a self-erasing code behind the ghost software. He came into the network employing adware. It doesn't appear to be malicious. Didn't you say he had a company?"

"Yes, Stealth Security."

"Did you see his web page?"

"Yes," Jennifer answered.

"He probably has a program to capture any visitor's email. Then he can follow up with an ad to that person a few days after the visit. It's an advertising thing, that's what adware does. I think he got your email from the dating site. He may have been able to sneak into their database, and capture all your information. Then he used his erasing software to go into your email, and that's how he found your son; the boy was using the Wi-fi in this house. Now, I'm going to go into his website, and find the server. It could be anyone; GoDaddy, Google, Yahoo, several servers do websites; it's all cloud tech. All of our information is collected, and stored in a warehouse in some Nebraska cornfield."

Jennifer and her mom looked at each other. They had no clue as to how Drake's tablet had a photo of Wendy. It was beyond their understanding, and impossible for them to visualize that occurrence linked to a cornfield in the Midwest. After an hour of watching Marshal mumble, and tap the keyboard, Jennifer went into the kitchen, and poured a mug full of coffee. She called to Marshal in the dining room. "Marshal, coffee?"

His eyes never left the screen. "Cream, and sugar, thanks."

"He's rather handsome, isn't he, Jen?" Beverly asked her daughter.

Jennifer was adding cream and sugar to a cup that read *The world's worst golfer.*

"He's a chocolate bar I'd like to lick."

Beverly shook her head. "So graphic. Don't you want to share a meal, and see a movie? Find out if he has children, things like that. I saw the way you two looked at each other. I felt like I was the third wheel in an X- rated movie. I blushed."

"It's called animal magnetism, mom. It's going straight to the matter, and getting the preliminaries out of the way. Once the sexual tension has been satisfied, you can genuinely have a conversation about likes, aspirations, and dreams. I know it seems backward to you, but that's what's going down in the world. A world I'm forced into because of Hunter. But all jokes aside, a second date is often when the deal gets closed. And it's not just the boy pushing the envelope; it's girls, too, mom. We're liberated, and work, and have the same wants, and desires, as the guys."

Jennifer smiled, gave her mom a coffee mug with cream and sugar, and a curtsey, then headed toward the dining room to serve Marshal. He was concentrating on the screens in front of him. When Jennifer set the cup down beside him, he looked up, and saw her as if it was for the first time. His brilliant smile pierced her, and she asked, rather slowly, with a smokey tone, "Would you like anything else?"

Marshal forgot what day it was, or why he was at the dining room table. Jennifer's large eyes, and sweet smile, flogged him into a fixed stare. His torso was leaning toward her, pulled by an unnamed gravity. He grabbed the table lip, and righted himself. "Ah, I can think of a hero's reward after I solve this mystery."

"You better get cracking, mister, because we don't have all day."

He smiled his brilliant smile, and returned to the two screens with renewed vigor.

Chapter 10

Hunter and Winston Markham were both stunned at the whirlwind of disasters spinning around them. Winston was on the phone with a detective agency, Marks & Hammel. He'd always heard good things about the agency, and he understood they weren't cheap. They'd turned the tide on some high-profile cases. After talking to the receptionist, Winston set up an appointment for early the next morning. He swallowed hard before he told Hunter they needed a $15,000 retainer.

Hunter looked anemic before his lawyer told him the cost. Now, his pale skin had a translucent outer layer. "Look, buddy," Winston said as he lowered himself into a chair facing Hunter in the living room. "These guys are topnotch, meaning they can sniff out this bastard Porowski, and find Valerie. We need the best, and we need them, now. I don't see these keystone cops with that asshole McDermott making Porowski their priority. They're focused on you. They can't wrap their heads around the fact that you might be innocent."

Winston and Hunter were asked by one of the forensic cops to leave the townhome. "It's an active crime scene."

Hunter asked if he could pack a suitcase. He was permitted by Mc-Dermott, and escorted up the stairs by a uniformed officer. "Hey," he said to the cop watching him, "my pistol is missing. I had a Glock 9 in the bedside drawer."

The cop called down the stairs. "Detective, this guy says his Glock is missing."

McDermott yelled up the stairs. "Confiscated on our first search. Illegally stored, not locked in a cabinet, and held for future reference in the disappearance of Steven Porowski."

Hunter groaned, and finished packing. He'd go to his father's house. In a crisis like this, a man needs someone on his side. Maybe they could figure out the best way forward. His every other thought landed on visions of Valerie. He couldn't stand the idea of Porowski smelling her skin, gazing into her beautiful eyes, and, God forbid, hurting her. In that mix of tortured thoughts, he knew he had to give Valerie some credit. She's smart as anyone, and not just book smart, or streetwise; she was brilliant. Under certain circumstances, he saw her escape, or talk to Steven about turning himself over to the police.

In the fog of all that occupied his mind, those two scenarios perked to the surface. One was aspirational, one was demonic. His helplessness was eating him like a stage four cancer, nibbling at his self-esteem, his inept ability to rescue the woman he loved. He had no idea where to turn. Winston drove; Hunter's car was impounded. His confusion, and fear, boiled off of him like steam. Before he pulled away from the curb, Winston reached out, and rubbed his friend's shoulder. "I'm so sorry this is happening, man. No one deserves a shit storm like this. I'll do anything I can to help you."

Hunter's muscular shoulders slumped, and he rubbed his red eyes. "That detective sucks. I mean, he keeps circling back to me. What a waste of time. And they took my gun. This investigation is making the facts fit the crime. It's driving an inquiry from a hunch based on a recording of me threatening Porowski. I noticed Steven edited the bit about my suggesting he get help, and about him being a hoarder. I pointed that out to McDermott, and he says, 'We have more blood loss on the floor than a human can survive, along with a video of you threatening that very person. Two plus two, equals four. Once a guy like him gets it in his head that somebody is guilty, he turns the entire case into supporting his belief. I thought these guys were supposed to follow the facts, and keep an open mind. Where's Valerie? That guy thinks I did something to her through osmosis. I was locked up when she was abducted. What an asshole."

"Well, buddy, we don't have to worry about him. You're out on bond. Keep your nose clean, and tomorrow we'll be talking to the best there is about finding Valerie, and Porowski. When they find him, they'll get Valerie back, and all the charges against you will be dropped. The receptionist told me they use a lab for forensic work on par with the FBI. I'm going to make a motion to get a sample of all the blood, and send it to them. Meanwhile, I'm going to be making some calls, and line up a defense lawyer. Homicide is not my expertise; you know that. I'm used to looking at the bad flashing around a chimney, and taking pictures from a drone."

"I don't know where I'd be without you, Winston. You're a true friend, and next time we're at the club, I'm going to give you all the mulligans I can."

"Okay, I'll remember that." The two men gave each other a weak, and slightly forced, smile. It was hard to glean any levity under the circumstances. Winston knew his way to Hunter's father's house. They'd been friends long before Hunter's mother died. Winston had spent a great deal of time playing pool in the Smithfield's dark, and humid basement. He dropped Hunter off, and told him he'd pick him up early in the morning. Watching his friend carry the suitcase toward the front door with his head lowered, and the weight of the world pulling him toward the ground, there was an assumption by Winston that the guy was probably beating himself up over leaving Jennifer, and his kids. His life wouldn't be a wreck if he'd stayed in the slow lane.

Hunter's father took one look at his son, and knew there was some serious trouble going on. The two went over everything that had happened. Once Hunter had finished explaining all of it, his father told

Hunter, "You did everything a man in your shoes would have done. You suggested to this guy that he needs to back off, and get help. And, if he didn't, you'd be back. It was a threat, but it was an idle threat. The cops are blind. As far as this girl Valerie, this is where the entire situation goes off the rails. It has nothing to do with Wendy. And, Drake, my God, he's just a child. So, we can't think in terms of cause, and effect. Normal doesn't apply in this case. We're outside the goal post on this one. Wendy set the ball rolling when she asked this guy Steven about his relationship with Abigail; a subject she knew nothing about that he brought up. She did the right thing leaving the guy at the restaurant. When you go tomorrow to this detective agency, I'll go and keep an eye out at the cemetery. It's not much of a lead, but something is something. There should be someone there who can point me to Abigail Porowski's grave. Once I've located it, I can keep watch."

Hunter called Jennifer to bring her up to speed as to what was going on. He also wanted to say hi to the kids. Hearing their innocent voices would be like touching an angel when you're trapped in hell. He was anxious, and that anxiety wasn't going anywhere until he had Valerie in his arms, safe and sound. Jennifer said she sent Detective McDermott a file. It's a copy, and verification of every ghost email Porowski had sent to her phone, Wendy's phone, Jennifer's email, and Drake's tablet.

"I told McDermott in the email I sent him that it's a crime to send pornographic material to a six-year-old. I'm waiting for a reply. It's evening now. I'm sure he won't see it until the morning."

Hunter finally felt a wave of relief. Things were beginning to point to Steven as the bad guy, and charges should be brought against him. But would McDermott continue to pursue him? That's the question of the day. He thanked Jennifer, and told her the cops had taken his gun, and kicked him out of his townhome, so he was at his dad's house. He then spoke to each of his children. He had tears streaming down his face as he told each of them how much he loved them.

When Jennifer got back on the phone, Hunter suggested that Jennifer's mom take the kids someplace away from Slate Shore, and go into hiding until they caught Porowski. "You remember Jen; he's yet to go after Wendy. So far, he's only punished me. He's sick, and there's no telling his motive for anything he's doing. I mean, Valerie isn't part of Wendy's family. It's just some random reaction to a bunch of garbled thoughts."

"I'll think about it, and talk it over with mom," Jennifer answered, then hung up. She was stinging with anger that Hunter had mentioned Valerie, yet, she's now a big part of the story, and in all honesty, she's probably going through hell, and no one deserves that. Jennifer needed to tone down her immediate reaction to the name Valerie. It'll be coming up a lot until they find her, or her body. Her knee jerk response wasn't helping her nerves. Besides, she had a dinner date with Marshal in fifteen minutes, and she needed to push all thoughts of Valerie out of her head.

STEVEN WAS MORE THAN pleased with the way things were going. He'd been scouting out a place to dump Valerie in the rural area at the base of Peach Mountain. Sitting off of route 17, at Gilberts Corner, inside a McDonald's, drinking hot coffee, and eating a cheeseburger, Steven happened to look into the parking lot, and saw a Loudon County cruiser blocking his van in a parking space. The cop was out of his car, looking into the back of the truck. Steven slowly stood up, and exited by the side entrance near the bathrooms. Then he moved into the woods behind the restaurant, and broke into a sprint.

He had every intention of ditching the van that very day. "Best of plans," he mumbled. He would keep moving until he came out at a used car sales, and gas station combo, some two miles from where he was now. It was a little past noon, and the weather on this side of the mountain was near record highs. He had to remove his windbreaker after running in the woods for less than ten minutes. He knew this side of the mountain was 20 degrees warmer than the dark side. The cabin holding Valerie had probably dipped into the upper 30's overnight. She had a large quilt that he placed over her for the night. He'd slept in the bedroom.

In his wallet, he had enough cash to buy a cheap car. He hoped to get a temporary tag, known as a ten-day-tag, and during that time, he could steal a set of tags, and be extra careful when he drove. His mind drifted back to the cop. If the McDonalds had a video of everyone who came and went, they'd have him buying his coffee, and burger. If that happened, they'd know Hunter didn't kill him. But if they didn't, they wouldn't have any idea of how the van ended up in the parking lot. He'd wiped it clean over the past two days, and he didn't think there was any evidence of Valerie being in the back of it.

Steven emerged from the woods as skittish as a deer. Looking both ways, he didn't see any cop cars. The parking lot of used vehicles outside of the gas station was mostly mid-sized, ten-year-old cars, with high mileage. The price of each hung from the rear-view mirror. He decided on a white Ford Taurus; a vehicle as bland as a glass of milk. The price was $950, and a half-hour later, he helped the owner install a ten-day paper tag.

Chapter 11

Valerie filled her mouth with water, and spat it on her wrist as a lubricant. She knew her strength was being siphoned, not only by the chelation treatment, but by lack of movement. It was now, or never. She pulled against the wire, and the Styrofoam pipe insulation. Valerie cried out in the cabin full of shadows as she felt a tug, her first sign of something positive since this nightmare began. She'd summoned all she had, and used her love of Hunter to give her strength. It was larger than herself; it was a struggle against every slight, every taunt, and twist, even slavery. Her cry was a clarion call to all those relatives who had freed themselves before her. Her wrist was pulling through the grip of the wire; it was moving, and her heart pounded.

"Oh, God, one more pull."

Steven noticed the smoke pouring out of the exhaust. His fear was a cop would pull him over. He turned onto a side street to let the engine warm the piston rings, and block the burning oil.

Her left hand was out. She wiggled the fingers in front of her eyes. "Stop wasting time!" She grabbed the hose with the needle sticking into her armpit, and jerked it free. A squirt of blood sprayed across the quilt. It stopped almost immediately. She rolled on her side, causing her waist to burn. She lifted the wire circle off the bedpost. She didn't spend any time loosening the wire, or the foam. With a foot of wire dangling from her wrist, she sat up, and leaned forward to her left foot. She spat water between her front teeth to gain distance. With both hands pushing for all she was worth, she was able to force the wire, and foam, to the back of her heal, and have it slip off.

She heard a car coming down the driveway. It had a different sound than the work van. No matter what, she had to assume it was him. Frantic, and in panic-mode, she grabbed the wire at the heel, and used her left foot to put pressure on the hands holding the wire. She didn't take the time to spray water; there was no lubricant. Adrenaline made up the difference. She heard a car door slam shut.

Steven climbed the three steps to the landing, and inserted a skeleton key. When the door swung inward, a ten-inch frying pan made of heavy iron connected with his face. He stumbled backward, and tripped over the lip of the landing where it dropped off for the top step. He landed on his back. To Valerie, he looked like he was knocked unconscious. She had no shoes, no socks, but the temperature had not yet registered. She leaned over Steven, digging in his pockets for the car keys.

His eyes flew open, and he grabbed her wrist with a death grip. She tried to shake him off. He held on, and was coming around, trying to stand while holding her wrist. Valerie screamed at his face, and headbutted his nose with her forehead. Blood shot out like a hose, and he let go of her arm. She stood up, and nearly passed out from a drop in blood pressure. She took one look at him, glanced at the sky, then took off running down the steep slope of the side of the mountain.

Sticks and rocks chewed into her bare feet. Each step was becoming painful. The hillside was populated with mountain laurel, bent, and soil starved ash, hickory, and locust trees. Her right hand flashed beneath her vision as the yellow wire danced with her arm. *He had shoes*, she told herself, *he can catch you*. She plunged forward, through briars of wild blueberry bushes, and blackberry thorns.

Suddenly, there was a steep drop, and she slid over rocks on her back. She felt something sharp dig into her spine. She screamed in pain, and when she stopped sliding, she saw a small creek. Valerie crawled to it, and drank all she could. She knew it was rich in minerals. Her mind conjured an image of a reservoir replenished. Then she heard a distant noise of dried leaves, and branches cracking above the shelf she'd just slid down. "Oh," she groaned, and stood on her bleeding feet, her back screaming with pain. She limped over the creek, and bent low as she disappeared into a grove of mountain laurel.

Steven tied a wet rag around his head, holding a couple of ice cubes against his nose. He'd pried up the loose board in the bedroom, and pulled out his grandfather's British Infield, a 303 bolt-action rifle used in world war two. He caught flashes of yellow in the bleak woods as he looked downhill toward Valerie, barefoot, and without a jacket, sprinting like a wounded deer.

He saw his victim bend into the laurel. He was even with her on this side of the little ridge. Steven decided he could hit her from where he stood. He raised the rifle, and shot where he thought she should be. He waited, and listened after the echo of the large-caliber gunfire dissipated. He heard her running. "Shit."

The good news was the woods turned into the Mathew Long National Forest. One of the many plots of land Virginia designated as parks. Hunting season was a month away, so the woods were empty. Porowski slid down the side of the crevice, and jumped across the creek. He clambered up the other side, and adjusted the cloth holding the ice on his nose. Every step pounded into his face. He had plans for Valerie; she'd rue the day she was born.

On the back burner, he realized he'd underestimated her. Abigail didn't escape. Neither did Mathew D'Angelo. And they'd tried; in front of him, behind his back, all the time they tried. But Valerie Washington had fooled him. He knew better, now. "A new plan, a quick one." A down and dirty bullet to the head. Later, when his face wasn't on fire, he'd bury her, and no one would be the wiser.

Valerie felt the cold forest floor. Every step was driving sharp obstacles up into the cut, and sore bottoms of her feet. Shivers came in waves of uncontrollable shaking. Her teeth rattled, and she wanted to sit and rest, and make a plan. She had no idea where she was, but she had an inkling that it was further north than the Maryland Eastern Shore. The sun was up, and high toward the west, and sooner, or later, it would go down. If nothing changed, she would sit, and fall asleep, and never wake up.

MCDERMOTT READ THE emails posted the night before from Hunter's wife. What difference did it make? It's justification for Hunter's anger, and going to Porowski's house, showing up on the video threatening the guy's life. The blood was still Steven's, and his car remained in front of his home. The problematic issue was the van, and that just showed up in Loudon County, Virginia. It had been wiped clean. Most likely by Hunter. A driver left it in the parking lot of a McDonald's. Unfortunately, the restaurant had a malfunctioning security system that was being repaired that very day.

"You're lucky," McDermott mumbled under his breath. He was thinking about Hunter, and how, once again, the guy had skirted any hard evidence. The detective prided himself on his sixth sense; his nose could smell it on the guy, once you got past the arrogant stench. He didn't like men who left their wives with children for a younger model. He and his mother, along with his two sisters, were abandoned by an alcoholic father. It cast a long shadow, and although Hunter seemed to remain engaged with his children, it was a scar on the children's lives, and his wife.

WENDY PUT THE KIDS to bed. Jennifer sent a text. "I'm getting jiggy with Marshal, be home tomorrow – smiley face – smiley face."

Beverly was floored. "My, God," she exclaimed to Wendy. "She's just met the man."

"Mom. She's at home all day with thoughts of Hunter and Valerie going at it with each other, and she's got no one."

"I bet she doesn't even know his middle name."

"Mom, who cares? It's not his middle name she's after. Wake up, and smell the sex. She's got a handsome guy, who happens to be very smart, giving her attention. She needs that mom; she didn't know if she was still desirable, or just some has been. It was eating her from the inside out. This fling will right a lot of wrongs. I know it's unorthodox, and it may seem a bit rushed, but I'm telling you that girl needed to get laid."

Her mother threw her arms out to the side, astonished at the turn of events all around her. "Is she taking precautions? I mean, all these venereal diseases don't go away. She could get something that could ruin her sex life, and maybe even threaten her life."

"Or," Wendy stopped, and held her mother's eyes, "she could have multiple orgasms, and scream like a banshee."

"What is a banshee, dear?"

"I have no idea, mom." Her mother turned away with her phone in her hand. "Mom, are you googling banshee?"

"Of course," she said without looking up. "Hmm, that's interesting."

"Okay, what is it?"

"It comes from Irish folklore; a supernatural being, a female spirit that lets out a moan when someone dies."

"I thought it was some obscure animal in the African jungle," Wendy said.

"I had the same belief," her mother said.

"Belief systems are made to be broken, Momma."

Beverly gave her daughter a sly smirk, one that conveyed the message, "You think you're so smart, don't you?"

Chapter 12

Hunter and Winston sat across the desk of Howard Long, a retired FBI field agent, who was recording their conversation, and jotting down things in a small notebook. "Do you know the name of the laboratory that sampled the blood?" Hunter and Winston looked at each other, then turned back to Howard, both shaking their heads no.

"Listen, blood is only suitable for 41 days, kept at the temperature of around 35 degrees. If it goes beyond that period, the red cells break down, and can't be used to help anyone. I need to get someone looking at the blood spill ASAP. Also, we need to interpret the crime scene, if there even was a crime. If it's just blood on the floor, that would be amateurish. If there are cast-off trails on the ceiling, and the walls, we need to see if it was staged."

Hunter interrupted Howard. "The walls had bloodlines, and so did the ceiling. It looked gruesome."

Howard bobbed his head, and adjusted his thick red tie. "We'll need to do a deep dive into this guy Steven Porowski. We need to talk to his customers, find out if he ever mentioned a fishing boat, if he liked to camp in the woods, anything to give us an idea of where he might be hiding out."

"He's a hoarder. I got the vibe that he was a loner. My wife found a poem he wrote to his dead sister." Hunter reached into his briefcase, and handed Howard a copy of the poem he'd written, and a document of all the emails he'd sent. "The image of my sister-in-law is photo-shopped. She's a nice-looking girl, but not so voluptuous."

"Why did he come after your girlfriend?" Long asked.

Hunter's eyes grew misty, and he shook his head. "I have no idea, other than to punish me for knocking him on his ass. And even then, I suggested he get help. I wasn't just some badass slamming him around. A part of me felt sorry for the guy. Maybe my humanity pissed him off. Nobody likes someone feeling sorry for them. I don't have a clue of why he'd kidnap Valerie."

Howard said, "It's displaced anger. Crazy people have strange motives. Let's hope we find Miss Washington soon, and safe." After he said that, Howard stood up, and added, "I'll send in Emily. She'll have you sign the contract, and take your deposit. I want to get boots on the ground today, like now. We don't have any time to waste. It sounds like this detective McDermott suffers from tunnel vision. That happens more than you know." Howard was gathering his tape recorder to leave the conference room, when he continued. "It's not only small-time dicks; this kind of thinking happens in big cities, too."

Hunter felt a weight lift off him as if passing a baton of worry over to Howard. "Thanks for hooking me up with that guy, Winston," Hunter said. Winston was concentrating on driving out of the city, and turned to Hunter at the entrance ramp to 495.

"No problem, buddy. That guy was all business. He seems competent as hell."

Hunter looked out the window at a concrete sound barrier, and said, "Yes."

VALERIE FELT AN ABSOLUTE clarity in thought. She attributed that to drinking from the mountain stream, and her body processing the metals, and minerals. At the same time, both of her feet were destroyed. Her strength, at its core, was drained. A vision from her childhood visited her mind. It was the end of summer, and Aunt Pearl, and Uncle Jake planned to kill a half dozen chickens, and put all except one in the freezer. Cricket was hopping around as usual. Uncle Jake explained that once you cut the chicken's head off, you hold onto them. If you let go, they'll bang into stuff, and when you freeze them, that place that got bruised will make the meat go bad.

Her uncle started a fire under a metal barrel cut in half, and filled with water. All the chickens except one were in a dog cage, out of sight. Uncle Jake had one large chicken in his hands. His fingers kept the feet together, and the other hand had a grip on the bird's neck. Cricket stumbled on one of his jumps, and banged into his dad. Uncle Jake dropped the bird, and Valerie watched as this sizeable white chicken stretched out its wings, slithered underneath a pile of leaves, and disappeared before her eyes. It looked like a magic trick. She needed to do that, and fast.

Limping, and jerking from the pain, Valerie moved as quickly as she could toward the crest of the nearby rise. Once she got there, she'd run down the other side, and begin covering herself with leaves, and pine needles. The brightest color on her was the yellow electrical wire cable. Other than that, she had an advantage over the chicken, which happened to be white. "It pays to be black," she mumbled, and smiled to herself.

Every step Steven made sent a jolt to his face; perhaps his nose was broken. He wasn't sure. The only thing keeping him going was his absolute need to kill Valerie Washington. He walked up the far side of the creek, his head swiveling back and forth for the slightest glimpse of movement. The bolt action on the rifle was making his hands cold. He shifted the gun. If he was cold, she had to be freezing. She had no shoes. The blouse she was wearing was flimsy. The black jeans she wore were filthy from her soiling herself. He wasn't going to risk taking her to the outhouse, or letting her sit up to use a bedpan.

All of his thinking moved him to a place of superiority. He had shoes, and a gun. It was only a matter of time before he found Valerie, dead, or near death. Maybe he'd toy with her for a little while, give her some hope, then take it away. The thought of dragging her death out with a bit of mental torture caused him to smile, which hurt like hell, and he stopped immediately. Walk, stop, listen, look, continue; that's how he moved closer to Valerie.

There was a crevice, a fissure in the lower side of the hill. The elongated dip was probably formed as runoff in the topsoil. The soil was hard to come by in this rocky terrain. The trees looked nutrient-starved on the shady side of the mountain. Valerie raked leaves, and twigs onto both sides of the scarred earth, approximately a foot deep. With a great sigh, she lowered herself down, stretched once, then she began pulling the debris over her. Once she had as much as she could on her face, and arms, she closed her eyes, and imagined twisting the exposed copper back and forth until it was warm. At that point, the wire would break. She could pull it out of the yellow sheathing, and use the vinyl to wrap pine branches around one foot. The wire could be used to bind pine branches at the bottom of her feet.

Her mother used to say, "Valerie, anyone can get to California. You head west, and don't stop until you hit the Pacific. But it's a lot easier with a map." It was her mother's way of telling her to make a plan. Now, she had a plan that would protect her feet. Later, after she rested, and regained some strength, she'd implement the plan. She needed more water, and God knows she could use some food. It was two days since she'd had anything to eat. Statue still, and lightly breathing, Valerie slipped into a deep sleep.

Hours slid into the past, and the sun pulled a curtain of darkness behind it as it winked out behind the woods, and took its warmth to the west coast. The night air condensed, and the isotopes tightened. The forest tensed, and under a bed of leaves, Valerie clenched her teeth to keep them from chattering. She thought if she didn't fight the desire to let her mouth vibrate, she'd chip and pound her teeth until they were nothing but nubs. Her arms shook. But it was her feet, those most outward extremities of her body, so far away from her heart, that felt like ice blocks, and she struggled to wiggle her toes. Just as she was beginning to stir, and work on her plan to wrap her feet in pine branches, and hopefully keep them warm and alive, she heard a branch snap.

In that briefest of moments when she had sat up, she saw a three-quarter, skim milk moon. It was bathing the forest in a kind of bleached light; a black and white world that would allow her to see, and also him. If he came close enough, he'd see her face resting on a pillow of moss, and leaves. *Would he speak first, or just put a hole in my head?* Deep down where the dark thoughts hide, she knew he could march her back to the cabin, strap her down so tight she couldn't move, then introduce her to the iron.

Another movement to her right. *Don't turn, don't let the moon reflect off your eyes. Keep still.* He was moving methodically, slowly, but he was making noise. She heard branches bend, then whip back again. She heard leaves pushed. It sounded like he was too tired to lift his legs. Maybe she could surprise him. She moved her hands in the hopes of finding a rock the size of a softball. She found pebbles. The desire to shake was coming to her from the cold earth that lined her back. Slowly, with her head mostly forward, she glanced to the right. Ten feet away was the white chest of a large deer. It was a buck with a ten-point rack.

It was intense, and majestic. She took it as a sign. As if this magnificent creature was guarding her. If there were a man around, this creature would be spooked, and moving away from the sound. It was a sign that she could come out, now, and start on her plan. She sat up. The deer raised its head, and stared at her. A sliver of the moon was painting a halo around its antlers, and for one moment, it seemed like it would come to her, and investigate. Then it changed its mind, and turned toward the bottom of the hillside, and broke through some thickets as it disappeared. Valerie rose as if from a crypt. She was now a nocturnal mammal; part possum, part vampire.

In the surreal light of the moon, she saw a straggling pine tree. On this, the dark side of the mountain, there were only short needle pine trees. The long, proud, and tall pines wanted the sun. They built a carpet of needles around their base to turn into mulch to feed the taproot. The short, and deformed pines on this side had their needles flushed away with each rain. Valerie wiggled the copper back and forth as she moved cautiously, and quietly toward the tree. The warmth of the copper was temporarily enjoyed as it rubbed into her palms before she returned to the business of breaking the wire.

Eventually, the wire broke, and she pulled it through the yellow sheathing. She was no longer tethered to it, and removed the pipe insulation from around her wrist. She had a white wire, a black wire, and bare wire in one hand. In the other was a six-inch piece of Styrofoam pipe insulation with the yellow wire insulation. She had plenty of supplies to tie pine branches around her feet. She broke branches for an intense, and cautious hour, then worked on fashioning the broken branches onto her feet. When the job was complete, she hugged her chest, rubbed her bare arms, and watched her breath make small clouds in the strange moonlight.

If it was daytime, and she was sure she was alone, Valerie believed she could take some of the vines dangling from the trees, and create a jacket out of mountain laurel, and pine branches. As long as she was dreaming, she might as well conjure up a three-course meal while periodically stopping to scan the woods for any movement, and listen for any noise. Suddenly, she stayed perfectly still. A light was weaving some distance to her left. *He must have gone back to the cabin for the flashlight.* She wasn't used to having her feet wrapped in pine branches. It was awkward, and they felt like snowshoes. But they were helping her have less pain. She turned right, and moved away from the light. Suddenly, she heard the bolt drive a bullet into the chamber, and she ran as fast as she could, zig-zagging as she went. *He must have seen me move.* Tears streamed down her face as she ran downhill. She felt the shoes falling apart. She'd be barefoot, again, in the night, with temperatures near freezing. The woods echoed with the sound of a bullet fired.

Chapter 13

Hunter filled Jennifer in on his meeting with Howard Long from the detective agency of Marks & Hammel. He told her he felt the retired FBI rep they met had experience, and was a real asset. Jennifer had a twinge of guilt when she reflected on her previous night-time extracurricular activities with Marshal. She and her mother had emailed all the information they had from his emails, and the poem, in a pdf file to Hunter before he went to Marks and Hammel. The same information they'd sent to McDermott.

Wendy was on the couch with bed hair, and had a faraway look. As Jennifer ended the call with Hunter, the first words out of Wendy's mouth were, "Poor Valerie."

Jennifer, in the same clothes she wore to have dinner with Marshal, agreed. The scenarios of what was happening to Valerie by Porowski were all sadistic. And the cops had their eye on Hunter. Were they even looking for Steven? Jennifer wanted a shower, one that would change everything, and make Valerie safe, but gone. Suppose she could scrub away the reality where Hunter loved her again, and didn't have a nest townhome somewhere. It was all so out of the left field. She couldn't wrap her head around any of it. If this pyscho was mad at Wendy, why didn't he attempt to kidnap her? Why Valerie?

Her kids were making cookies with their Grandma. Wendy was half awake, and on her way to find coffee. Now was a good time for Jennifer to take a shower, and regroup. Drift just a little bit, and relive some of the action in Marshal's hotel room. They were going to see each other again, even though it was difficult with the distance between them. She felt they'd had a connection, especially after telling him what was going on with her husband, and the abducted mistress, Valerie.

He suddenly had an understanding of Jennifer's flirtation. He was recently divorced, and missed the closeness he had with his four-year-old daughter. He told her it felt surreal, even today. They commiserated over their supposed dreams, and aspirations, vanishing before their eyes. Marshal's situation was sudden, and strange. His wife had fallen for another woman she'd met at the gym. She confessed to Marshal it was always there, that pull, and when she acted on it, she'd felt like she was honest with herself, and the world, for the first time.

"Where did that leave me?" he'd asked Jennifer.

It was the confluence of mutual sympathy that caused them both to recognize each other as damaged goods. The light-hearted sexual tension, and attraction, took a tender turn into the realm of support with gentle accolades. "You're handsome," followed by, "You're beautiful." In the shower, Jennifer felt selfish for her recent sorbet. Poor Valerie; she may be tied up, and being tortured. Is it because she was a homewrecker? Is that why Steven went after her, to make her pay for her sins? How convoluted is that? Wendy had opened the can of worms, and has only suffered a few emails.

Meanwhile, Hunter's charged with Porowski's possible death; Valerie's missing, presumed tortured, but only by their family unit. The cops still think Hunter's behind everything. How can that even be? The turn of events dumbfounded Jennifer. They've searched Hunter's house, office, and car. He had a witness, a lawyer for God's sake, and McDermott has yet to admit that Valerie has been stolen like a piece of jewelry. Is he entertaining the idea that Hunter had an accomplice, or that Valerie staged her disappearance?

To what purpose? Jennifer thought. What would be gained by either scenario? Hunter told her that he loved Valerie. Why would she surreptitiously go missing? As she was drying her hair, and trying to make sense of what was going on, Wendy knocked on the bathroom door, and said, "Hey, mom says breakfast is ready."

Jennifer opened the door with a brush in her hand, and told Wendy she'd be right there. As she walked the hall toward the kitchen, she couldn't shake the feeling that there was a tornado swirling around her, the kids, Wendy, and her mom, and it was destroying everything in its path, and they were somehow immune to its wrath. Not that she wanted any more drama, it was just a pitiful empathy for Hunter, and Valerie. Even though she hated them for destroying her world, she already saw a glimpse of what her future looked like, and if it was anything like the incredible physical, and emotional highs of last night, she was okay with it.

"Is that a glow on your skin, Jen?" Wendy asked in a teasing way, especially in earshot of her mother, whom she liked to freak out.

"Maybe," Jennifer answered with a smile.

Beverly was setting the table with a breakfast that glistened, and beckoned both children, and adults, alike. There was a plate full of bacon, another with whipped scrambled eggs, and a stack of pancakes. The two daughters were used to yogurt, and a multigrain piece of toast without butter. The stress of all the unprecedented events circling their wagon made them dig in, and show their appreciation to their mother.

When the children had finished, and moved to the rec room to turn on the cartoon channel, the three women cleared the table. Beverly asked out loud what all of them were thinking. "Do you think Valerie is still alive?"

It was a question that plagued their dreams; a watery scene with a woman tied to a post that swirled in shadows, only to leave an uneasy impression. A mental bruise that wasn't going to heal until there were answers. While it was a concern to them, they knew it was shredding Hunter, as every minute passing must be an exercise in frustration. Was there more they could do? They talked about the emails, and their connection to Porowski. Wendy and Jennifer had no confidence in the lead detective, McDermott.

Beverly asked for the detective's business card, and she said she'd give him a call. It was, after all, her grandchild who had received the pornographic photograph. She wanted to know what, if anything, was being done to find, and stop this Steven Porowski from sending more filth to her six-year-old grandson. Wendy and Jennifer encouraged her. Their mom took the card, and sat down at the table, still wet from a washcloth, and called McDermott.

MCDERMOTT WAS GETTING pressure from a big city detective agency, Marks & Hammel. An ex-FBI guy by the name of Howard Long wanted access to Porowski's house. He needed a sample of blood sent to a lab that would do a thorough analysis. He needed his people to view the crime scene, and document the cast-off trails. He let McDermott know they would be forensically assessing the evidence on behalf of Hunter Smithfield, and his lawyer, Winston Markham. Long also asked McDermott if there was any news as to where Porowski might be hiding.

"We're under the assumption," Shawn McDermott began, "that Steven Porowski has suffered a fatal injury. The amount of blood at his home suggests that no one could bleed out that much, and survive. His car is in front of his house, and his work van has been discovered abandoned in a McDonald's parking lot in a rural section of Virginia. We're assuming it was stolen; there were no security cameras to tell us anything, one way, or another. It appears to have been wiped clean. So, yes, we're looking for Steven Porowski, and by that, I mean we're doing our best to retrace the steps made in recent days by Hunter Smithfield."

Howard arranged a time that his people could go to Porowski's home. Shawn hung up, and ran his hands through his hair; a habit in times of stress. After receiving the pdf file from Jennifer Smithfield, he'd thought it only added to the case against Hunter; the reason for Porowski's murder. But there was also a nag in the back of his head. It wasn't insightful enough to change the direction he was moving in with the investigation; it was an acknowledgment that Steven was spiteful, and devious. And that could spill over into blood.

Not wanting to be outflanked, McDermott called the laboratory that had checked the DNA on the pool of blood in Porowski's home. He specifically asked them to make sure there wasn't anything funny about the blood. Shawn voiced his suspicion of a possibility that the crime scene was staged. The technician he spoke with assured the detective that he'd check it for any anomalies. No sooner was the phone hung up; it rang. The detective picked it up. "McDermott," he answered.

"Detective, this is Beverly Valise. I'm Jennifer Smithfield's mother, and the grandmother of six-year-old, Drake Smithfield. I'm calling for an update on the arrest of Steven Porowski for sending pornographic material to a child." After her pronouncement, Beverly was still, and silent.

"Mrs. Valise, this is an ongoing investigation, and I'm not at liberty to divulge any information at this time. If, for any reason, your grandson, daughter, or son-in-law have any contact with Porowski, let me know immediately. Other than that, I can assure you we're looking into several avenues in this situation. As you can guess, we're pretty busy around here, right now, so I'm sure if something significant surfaces, Hunter will let you know. Good day, ma'am," and with that, the detective ended the conversation.

AFTER BEING CALLED in for a second opinion, Raymond Lewis stretched, and set his suitcase on the lawn of Steven Porowski's run-down home. He took his time while an officer patiently waited on the door stoop. Out of his Volkswagen Jetta, Ray retrieved a Tyvek suit, booties, and gloves. He took his time adjusting a half-mask respirator with the purple filter for tiny particles, and a charcoal layer for any biological threat. The officer on the stoop stared in amusement as the forensic technician finished suiting up with a hood, and goggles. Lewis listened to his breath. It felt like he was underwater.

The officer nodded, and swung the door open. Ray entered the home, and immediately looked at the pool of dried blood on the floor, and the cast-off trails on the walls, and ceiling. Raymond was a certified blood pattern analyzer. His expertise was crime reconstruction, specifically in the area of all things blood. After viewing the site, he went back outside, and grabbed a small step stool with a large standing platform. He would need to prove what he immediately suspected.

The dynamic forces that send blood to a ceiling are generally associated with a knife. A bullet tends to leave its mark on a wall. With string line analysis used on a ceiling, certain information can be gleaned. From the beginning of a cast-off trail, to the spray's furthest drop, measurements can be determined, and concluded in distance, and force. Measuring the ceiling's height is the final number used to plug into a Hemostat computing system. The computer uses a tangent trigonometric formula that automatically calculates the angle of the dynamic force. It used to take Raymond hours with a calculator to do what his new program did in minutes.

He took multiple photographs of the string lines, and the measurements beside them. It took him three hours to finish all his work on the ceiling. Looking around at the house, the owner was an apparent hoarder. He was glad he had the charcoal filter, so he didn't have to smell anything in the house. He assumed it stunk. He stepped outside, and removed his mask, and goggles. He went to the police cruiser, and spoke to the officer now sitting in his car.

"I'm done with the ceiling. I need to feed a bunch of numbers into my computer, then start on the walls. I'll do the floor last. If I give you my card, can you order us both something to eat for lunch?"

"How do you feel about seafood?" The cop asked.

"I'll eat anything you get us, and my company pays for everything, so don't hesitate to get us something good."

The police officer looked like he'd hit the lottery as he began thumbing through his phone for places that delivered. Raymond found that buying cops a good lunch went a long way into ingratiating himself with the locals. He set his laptop on the hood of the Jetta, and leaned over to type in all the information he had from the ceiling. It wasn't long before he had a basic idea for reconstructing the events that made the ceiling pattern.

The first V-shaped cones had an angle beginning six inches below the ceiling, or ninety inches off the floor. The evidence showed that someone approximately six-feet tall, with their arm extended, flung blood nearly parallel with the ceiling to appear as if someone had suffered a vicious attack. There were cross-contamination areas, yet the trails consistently originated from a near-vertical projection. The scene was an amateurish attempt to give the appearance of a fatal event. Raymond called Howard, and told him he'd continue to drive home the point with more illustrations. He would also cut out portions of the floor in several areas for the laboratory, but he wanted to check for linear striations before sending the samples to the lab.

Howard said one word. "English."

Ray smiled. "If the blood wasn't poured onto the floor all at one time, then I should be able to, under a microscope, see the different layers."

"That's fine work, Ray, keep it up." Howard put the phone down, and called Shawn McDermott. The detective's phone was answered on the second ring.

"McDermott."

"Detective, my blood pattern analysis specialist, using the latest tools, including a computer system to calculate dynamic force, and angle of splatter, says the blood was flung at the ceiling from the extended arm of someone approximately six-feet tall. The blood consistently looked to be sent at an angle that was vertical to the ceiling. There were no cast-off lines that traveled the wall, and ended in the ceiling. The blood was in the opposite pattern of a true-crime scene, and went from the ceiling to the wall. I'm not sure why your guys didn't pick that up, but Porowski didn't die in that house."

There was a long pause on the detective's end of the phone, then he spoke. "The guy we nailed for the murder is a smart man. He could have staged this with the blood of Porowski, knowing an intelligent organization like yours would come along, and call foul. I'll keep everything you've told me in mind as our investigation continues."

Howard Long could hardly believe his ears. He spoke slow, trying to keep a lid on his anger. "Don't let a young woman die because you couldn't admit you made a mistake. We all make mistakes. No one is infallible. If that happens, if you know where he might be, and you don't follow up on that, I will make it a life's crusade to see you're held personally responsible for whatever happens to Valerie Washington. And you better not get within striking distance of me if you let this ball drop."

McDermott said, "I'm sure you're aware that threatening a law enforcement agent is a crime."

Long said, "I'll tell you what a crime is, McDermott. Letting a woman die because you were too fucking stubborn to admit you were wrong." Howard Long ended the call.

Chapter 14

Wendy took a shower after overeating food at breakfast. Thoughts of Valerie plagued them all. She was mad at Hunter for the pain he'd caused her sister by moving in with Valerie. But being angry, and having poor Valerie taken, and under the control of crazy Steven, didn't fit in the same paragraph. Women and men working together, day, after day, often fall in love. That's an old story. A minute later, she thought about what Jennifer told her about Marshal, and his wife leaving to be with another woman. Relationships are tough.

It was inevitable that when her thoughts circled the wagon of relationships, she drifted back to Ray. "I was just a box you checked." Maybe that's the key; don't take things for granted. If, and when, she's in another partnership, she's going to remind herself to say lovely things in the middle of washing dishes, and call him at ten a.m. on a workday to tell him she appreciates him. If nothing else, Ray has given her that. And for her, that's a significant clue.

With her wet hair wafting the shampoo's fragrance at the kitchen table, Wendy asked her mother and sister if they knew that the State of Maryland owned the Potomac River. The two women didn't. "Well, when I was in Westmoreland county searching for information on Porowski's relatives, this lady told me people come to Colonial Beach because it has gambling. But, because Virginia doesn't have gambling, the casino is located in the river, and that the state of Maryland owns the river."

Beverly said, "I wish we had some information to help that poor girl. I can't imagine what's going through Hunter's head." Her mother looked at her daughter, Jennifer, and said, "I'm sorry, dear, but it is what it is."

"I know, mom," Jennifer replied. "I think about her, too. I doubt she's still alive."

Wendy said, "That's what I was thinking, but I didn't want to say it."

"I like to have hope," Beverly began. "It's often the only thing that keeps us going. And because I have hope, I try and send Valerie any strength that I can through whatever mechanism such things happen. Let's not give up on her. On some level, I believe we're all connected. To what extent, who knows."

Wendy and Jennifer glanced at one another, feeling somewhat chastised. "Okay, mom, that's an excellent way to proceed. When I think about Valerie, I'll try and send her some of my strength for her to stay alive."

Jennifer acquiesced with a nod of her head to both her mother, and sister. Perhaps sending positive vibes toward Valerie would become part of a healing process, and acceptance of the inevitable; that she and Hunter had no future. Because if Valerie were dead, she wouldn't want him back. "You're only back because your girlfriend is dead." How horrible that sounded, but thoughts come and go, and that one had some validity to it. He left her once, and she would never again be secure with him. She'd had friends who tried to remain a couple after one of them was unfaithful. They stayed together for the kids, or financial reasons.

She'd watched as they'd lied to themselves that this would ultimately strengthen their resolve. It didn't work. Life has stress, and when pressure is applied to something already a little shaky, the cracks start to appear. Hunter listened to him, and she listened to her when friends of theirs would fight. In the end, she and Hunter decided they needed distance from the fractured couple because it was affecting their marriage. The broken couple brought up contagious issues. "We don't make love as often. He doesn't listen. She doesn't try to be sexy. All he talks about is work. The kids are a job, too, but he dismisses it as if it's a hobby that'll never pay off."

Jennifer and Hunter saw themselves in the fighting couple's complaints. They did their best to adjust, and distance themselves from couples who were going through a rough patch. They'd gone to a marriage counselor for advice. The woman they saw took them back to the beginning, to the genesis of their falling in love. Jennifer and Hunter remembered those early days. They'd left the councilors office smiling, and laughing about the good old days. There was a return of passion to the bedroom. And then, slowly, gravity did its job. The sun followed its course. Birthdays came, and went; Hunter fell in love with Valerie.

If Jennifer was honest, it hadn't been all that great for a few years. It wasn't that Valerie had snatched Hunter out from a Norman Rockwell painting. They'd become robotic, memes representing two people that had settled. Jennifer was herself with Marshal, and she'd let him seduce her because for more reasons than getting even with Hunter, she needed an on-ramp to her new life. So, she could send any strength she had using her mom's magical thinking. Because it was slowly becoming clear that her life was going to turn toward a more fulfilling existence, and for that, she had Valerie to thank.

"Let's look over all the information we have," Jennifer suggested. "Going back, before your first date with Steven. Wendy, can you think of anything he said that might help us find that freak?"

Wendy's hair was still damp from the shower; it clung to her scalp, and it made her look ten years younger. She nodded her head as if Jennifer had a good point. She closed her eyes, and thought back on their conversations. "I remember he said he liked the woods. That listening to the wind in the trees was therapeutic."

Beverly said, "Why don't we bring all the emails he sent, the poem from the cemetery, and the genealogical information. We'll spread it out on the dining room table, and go over everything with a fine-tooth comb."

The kids were in the basement; Jennifer checked on them, and made sure they were alright. She'd called Slate Shore Elementary school, and told the secretary that Drake would be out for a while; he had a low-grade fever. The idea of leaving the children anywhere at this point was a nonstarter. A crazy man is running around kidnapping people. The same guy that sent her six-year-old a naked picture of his aunt. Until there's a resolution in terms of his arrest, she couldn't risk taking Drake to school.

HOWARD LONG CALLED Hunter, and assured him the pool of blood, and the cast-off trails, were all staged. He told his client about his conversation with Detective McDermott. He expressed his contempt for the detective. As they talked about the case, Hunter informed Howard that his mother-in-law, and wife, had downloaded some ancestry information. He continued to explain that his sister-in-law had followed up on any property that Porowski's relatives might have left Steven in a will. That went nowhere. Long asked if they could fax, or email all the information they had to him. Hunter said he's on it.

Hunter was happy to have something to do. He hadn't slept, and was walking around his father's house talking to himself. When he called, Jennifer said they had all the documentation in front of them. She took the investigator's information, and promised Hunter she'd send a copy to him. Beverly didn't know that her printer could also scan. Her daughters showed her how it worked. Long and Hunter had a copy of the file in their email. After that, they went back to the dining room table, and spread the information out, once again. They developed a system where Beverly looked at each page, and passed it on to Wendy, who then handed it to Jennifer.

It wasn't until they had the article of Steven shooting his first deer that they had a group epiphany. "This is the clue," Beverly waved the paper. It made its way around the table. Jennifer and Wendy made some hasty plans. They'd ride together to the courthouse in Burlington County, and look up the property that Steven's uncle had owned. Then they'd casually drive by the house, and see if there's any activity.

Soon, the two sisters were following the GPS toward Burlington in rural Virginia. Once they cleared the toll booths, and Dulles Air-Port, the land began to roll, and gave way to some beautiful vistas of rock stacked fencing that dated back to the times of slavery. Cattle had trimmed the fields to landscape perfection. It was a breath of fresh air for both girls as they needed to see something new, and inspiring.

The courthouse had an ancient stone façade with brick walls lining the side, and back. They parked in the rear of the building, and were soon directed into the hall of records. Not knowing the lot number, and location, was making the microfiche task nearly impossible. The clerk suggested they go to the local paper, the Burlington Bugle, and ask them for help.

The paper's headquarters was a block away. Lucky for Jennifer and Wendy, the owner was sitting behind his desk when Wendy showed him the article, and explained they were searching for the boy's uncle's property. "Believe it or not, I remember that story. I believe the property you're looking for is on Peach Hill. Go back to the courthouse, and ask Lydia to give you the records for that subdivision. There's not much of a turnover on that hill. Folks around here don't die too far from where they were birthed."

Before going back to the courthouse, the ladies stopped in at a popular lunch eatery, and were soon eating the meatloaf special. Wendy googled Peach Hill while they waited for the food. The mountain was twenty minutes away. She sent a text to their mother to tell her where they were, and what they planned on doing next. They ate mostly in silence. The food tasted homemade, and cost very little for such a heaping plate of string beans, mashed potatoes, and meatloaf.

Back at the courthouse, Lydia gave them one roll of microfiche. It didn't take them any time to find lot 14 on the far side of Peach Hill. A map on the wall of the entire county showed them where lot 14 began, and ended. Wendy took a picture with her phone, and sent the information to her mother. They could reference the map, and her mother would know where the girls were should anything nefarious happen.

In the back lot, Jennifer started their mother's car, and the two looked at each other with solemn faces. "This is the real shit, Jen," Wendy said.

"I know, and there's no use taking any unnecessary risk. We have to remember Steven's crazy, and if he got his hands around your neck, Wendy, I think he'd snap it." Wendy swallowed, and gave a slight nod.

Chapter 15

Valerie had a cascade of thoughts that rained down from the wrong place. Was this the price she had to pay for stealing change as a teenager? Maybe she deserves what's happening because she took a married man away from his family. Her strength was draining out from beneath her ruined feet. The ground crunched from the crisp leaves covered in ice-cold dew. She wondered what he'd seen from so far away to make him shoot in the moonlight. Maybe it was just her moving that caught his eye.

It was all she could do to create some distance between the two. And as the sun was soon to rise with hints beyond the tree line of the first glimpse, she saw the straight edge of a roofline. Valerie limped, and struggled to reach the house, and hopefully get help. But as she got closer, she could tell it was a ranger's building; dark and empty. A notice board filled with stapled pages of various dates for hunting deer, turkey, and bear, were on the board. Valerie took her elbow, and broke a windowpane on the front door. She reached in, and grabbed the door handle.

Inside, the room was dark, but with just enough light to show a desk, a cot with a couple of blankets, and a kitchen with only a few cans of soup, and beans. She wrapped four cans in a handful of blankets, and left the cabin, closing the door behind her. There was a road to her right; a gravel road that went toward civilization. The structure was elevated, and she saw a foundation vent. Walking around to the back of the place, she saw an access door. It was two feet wide, by a foot tall. Valerie opened it, and the door swung out toward her. She tossed in the blankets, and the cans of food. It wasn't easy. She twisted, and squeezed into the crawl space, pulling the little door closed behind her. Inside it was tight. The blankets, and cans were slowly dragged to the furthest corner.

Valerie lay down with her head pressed into musty dirt. Only by inches was she able to pull the blankets under her, and around her feet. Two of the cans had pull tops on them. She opened one, and drank in chicken broth, and noodles. When she finished, she closed her eyes, and held onto the second can. Then she heard feet moving on the front porch. The door above her must have swung open. She heard boards creaking inches above her face. The feet moved like a human animal; two steps forward, stop, and then perhaps he was smelling to see if he could pick up her scent.

Valerie began to shake, and she did her best to make sure her fear didn't give her away. He has no idea she's under him at this very moment. The noise of him walking around the structure continued. He was hesitant, cautious, and quiet. He opened and closed cabinet drawers, and doors. If Steven found her under the cabin, what would he do? She couldn't stand the thought of being tied back to that bed. But she was so weak, and tired, there wasn't much she could do about any of it.

She began to feel a small sense of pride in having broken his plan. She would die fighting to be free. It was in her blood. There were oral stories of her relatives leaving slavery, and joining the negro army of the union. That part of her, some unnamed essence, was passed down through blood for this occasion. Those poor slaves must have been frightened, but also extremely brave. She needed some of that bravery, now. He was on the porch, perhaps looking down the road, and wondering if she was following it. That's what she thought, anyway.

Then there was silence. Where did Porowski go? She sank into the stale smell of the blankets. They were woolen, and itched, but were also warm. She felt the can of food inside her being converted into energy. Her eyes were closed when she heard the access door creek open. She was shaking so bad she thought her teeth would give her away. But Steven was bone tired. He only passed the light in the immediate area without getting on his knees, and looking into every space. The ground didn't look like someone had recently dragged themselves into the crawl space. It was dusty. He rested his hand against the wall of the building, and breathed slowly. She heard him breathing, and she wanted to scream. He was regaining his strength. He needed to go back, get his car, and drive down the road very slowly. He barely shut the access door, leaving it open a few inches.

He jogged when he had a spurt of energy. The sun was up, and he was familiar with the woods. Even though he wanted to exact pain on Valerie, he had admiration. Maybe he'd give her a break, and end her misery with one shot to the heart, put her down like a rabid animal. Back in the house, he drank water, and made coffee. With a thermos full of hot coffee, and a bag of snacks, he got in his piece of crap car, and warmed it up until it stopped smoking. Then he drove down Peach Hill, then onto a side road until he arrived at the state park's eastern entrance.

A hundred feet in on the gravel road, he poured a cup of coffee, and ate some peanut butter cookies. Valerie didn't know he had a car; all she'd seen was a van. If he was at a distance, and she saw the Taurus, most likely, she'd wave for him to help. And that would be the end of his escaped victim. Hunter would be wondering for the rest of his life what happened. It would torment him, and probably send him into therapy; the kind he recommended that Steven should find. He smiled, and it hurt his face because he had a damaged nose.

WENDY WAS APPREHENSIVE when they crossed over the crest of the mountain, and into the shade. It was colder, and the trees seemed a little more twisted. This side of the hill felt like it was caught in a different time. One where electricity was still scarce, and people didn't take kindly to outsiders sticking their noses in places they don't belong. She squirmed in her seat, and fastened her button-down one more button up. As if to give the image of a good Christian woman with a healthy dose of God-fearing joy. And there was fear; every switchback gave a glimpse into a deep drop off.

"If these roads were ice-covered from rain freezing, no one could drive in, or out," Jennifer said.

"This place gives me the creeps; it's like the sun has never shown on this side of Peach Hill," Wendy replied. They'd both felt like they'd entered no man's land. Like some hillbillies could drag them off into a cave, and no one would say what happened. They'd continue to whittle little figurines for Christmas presents, or to sell at a flea market. Suddenly, they saw the turn-off to a crushed slate driveway. They could see recent tire marks. Wendy blurted out, "I have no signal; we're on our own."

Jennifer stopped the car, half in the driveway, and half in the street, and said, "Suppose we're like ten minutes from saving Valerie."

"Well, Jen," Wendy said, "let me hold the gun while you drive."

"It's in the glove box. I thought the courthouse would have a metal detector, but they didn't even have a guard."

"Maybe we weren't in the section that held court."

"That makes sense," Jennifer said as she eased off the road, into the driveway.

Wendy had the gun in her hand, ready to shoot if need be. "Stop, Jen, don't go any further until you tell me something about this gun."

Jen showed her the safety switch, and told her how it worked. She retracted the feed, and sent a bullet into the chamber. Then she flipped the toggle on the side, so the gun was on safety. "All you need to do is flip that thing to the right, and it's ready to shoot."

Wendy held onto the gun with two hands, like she'd seen on television, as Jennifer continued down the driveway. "Do we know what kind of car he's driving?"

"We're here to see if Valerie is in his house, and free her, and kill Steven if we have to," Wendy said, never taking her eyes off the view in front of her.

The sound of the tires crushing the crumbled up soft stone under its weight was the only noise they heard. Around a slow curve, they could see a small one-bedroom house up ahead. It had a yellow bug light shining on the front porch. Jennifer said, "Damn, they got electricity to this place."

"I bet they don't have indoor plumbing," Wendy said as her hands were leaking buckets onto the trigger mechanism of the pistol.

There was no car, no van, or truck. It was just the two sisters. Jennifer said. "You can't walk up to someone's house holding a pistol, Wen."

"Well, I'm not getting out of this car without it," Wendy said as she scanned the area in front of her as if she'd just entered Fallujah.

Jennifer said, "Mom's got one of her shawls on the back seat; cover it with that."

Wendy draped the colorful shawl over her arm. It was a yellow and red affair that was fall colors, and Wendy caught a hint of her mother's perfume. "This thing smells like mom."

Jennifer stood off to the side, not wanting to expose too much of herself as she knocked on the front door. They waited an eternity. Then she turned the handle, and the door swung inward. What should have been the living room had a bed with wires hanging from some of the bedposts. There was a pouch with some yellow stuff on the left side floor. It had a tube sticking out of it, and was attached to a needle, and some loose tape. The room smelled of urine, and shit. There were traces of blood on the dirty sheet.

At the kitchen sink was a rag with blood on it. Wendy touched it. It was still wet. She felt the coffee maker. It was warm. She pulled the gun out from the shawl, went to the backroom, and flipped on the light. There was a bed, and a dresser—men's clothing strewn all over the place. Wendy turned to find Jennifer inches behind her. "I think Valerie might have been tied down to that bed, and either died, or escaped."

"What do we do, now?" Wendy felt inept.

Jennifer said, "Let's go find cell service, and call Hunter."

As they turned around to leave the bedroom, they heard a car door slam. Wendy said, "Jen, you hide in this room. I'll go see who's out there."

Wendy looked out the kitchen window, and saw Steven aiming a rifle at her face. She dropped just as a bullet shattered the glass. Screaming, Wendy raised the gun in the air, and shot toward where Steven might be standing. She pulled the trigger, but nothing happened. He fired again, and this time, he was shooting through the wall. Wendy yelped, and crawled to the front door. Along the way, she remembered the safety switch on the pistol. Her thumb flicked the safety to the off position. When she crawled to the back bedroom, she saw the window was open, and Jennifer was gone. The front door banged open. Wendy sent three quick shots in the general direction of the door.

The large rifle returned fire, and splinters flew all over the room. The mirror above the dresser sent shards of glass flying. Wendy believed she'd sustained wounds several times, but it was just debris hitting her back, and legs. *Don't just shoot, aim; aim at him before you pull the trigger.* It was a sobering command. She looked down the hall at the front door from the bedroom floor, and didn't see anything moving. Suddenly, a rifle came in through the open window of the bedroom, shooting blindly.

The window was taller than Steven could reach, so he raised the rifle above his head, and sent a shot, brought it back to his hands, and used the bolt action to send another bullet into the firing chamber.

Wendy aimed at the hand holding the rifle, and pulled the trigger, hitting something; the gun, or his hand, or both. The firing stopped, and she heard Porowski cussing on the far side of the wall. Wendy ran out the front door, and down the driveway past her mother's car. When she ran by Steven's car, she saw Valerie unconscious in the back seat.

She looked dead, but Wendy saw her chest move. She opened the white Taurus' back door, and nudged Valerie with her hand, gently rocking her back and forth. "Valerie, wake up."

Chapter 16

Valerie had slept for a few hours under the ranger's cabin. Then she'd eaten the second can in the crawl space. This time, she chewed on beans, and it was delicious. When she'd finally come out, scooting backward through the access door, she met a bright sun. Slipping into the ranger's kitchen, she grabbed a can opener, and some more cans of food. She found a rusty steak knife, and took these treasures into the woods on the opposite side of the road.

Valerie used the knife for ripping the blanket into strips with new hope, and energy, and she tied the cloth around her feet. Some good things were happening to her. She was no longer hungry, but she was thirsty. The canned food was laden with salt. She swallowed with a dry mouth, picked up some leaves, and licked the moisture off of them. Slowly, she realized that she'd met her immediate needs. No longer cold, hungry, or thirsty, a sliver of optimism rose within her spirit, and Valerie made a plan.

Her exit from the wilderness into civilization would be to move very slowly with the blanket wrapped around her shoulders covered in leaves, and twigs. She'd follow the gravel road until it met asphalt, then she'd take it from there—one step at a time. There was freedom within her grasp.

However, absolutely nothing can be assumed, or taken for granted. Porowski was a determined psychopath, and his drive came from some demonic force that stirred his brain chemicals into a wild soup, hell-bent on killing her.

Valerie stayed low, slightly bent, and moving like a cautious deer. Two steps forward, slowly move her head, then repeat. As she went eastward, she heard the sound of traffic, a distant truck as it shifted gears, and the hum of multiple cars. It came in snatches carried by a favorable wind encouraging her to continue. The sun winked between trees as if to say, you can do this. The planets had aligned, and the stars followed suit. Two steps forward, stop, and become aware.

She saw the white Taurus four-door coming slowly down the gravel road. Steven had a van, not a white sedan. Caution be damned, she ran from the woods to the road, and waved her arms. Porowski stepped out of the car, and aimed the rifle at her head.

"You came close," he said. "But not close enough."

He walked to where she stood. She closed her eyes, expecting to be shot point-blank in the head. Porowski swung the butt of the rifle into her temple, and she dropped like a stone. He struggled to get her into the back of the car. Feeling like a winner, he drove back to the little house in the woods.

He saw an unfamiliar vehicle. He stepped out with the rifle at the ready. That's when he saw Wendy, the bane of his existence, peering through the glass at him. He fired too quickly; he hadn't taken proper aim.

JENNIFER HEARD THE gunshot, and ran to the window. She slid out of it on her stomach. It was a bit of a drop, and she fell backward, hitting her head so hard, it hurt in her stomach. Staggered, she rose to her feet, and ran down the side of the mountain as fast as she could. Thoughts of her sister pelted her as she slowed, and reconsidered. It wouldn't do anyone any good if they were both dead. Was that her excuse? Could she live with herself for abandoning Wendy? But she had children. Wendy was single.

She couldn't just run away. It already weighed her down. Jennifer tossed her shoulders back, and moved horizontally, far from the structure, and deep into the scraggly forest on the left side. Once she caught sight of the roofline, she dropped to her knees, and crawled forward, trying to make as little noise as possible.

Porowski had his rifle aimed at Wendy's head. She dropped the pistol as she retracted herself from leaning into the car, trying to wake Valerie. "You think you could come out here by yourself, and kill me, and rescue that home-wrecking whore? What an inflated ego you have." Wendy was out of the backseat, standing in front of Steven. He was taller than she'd remembered, and his hand was covered in blood with a rag tied around it. His fingers were free, and he could hold the rifle with his index finger on the trigger. His nose was damaged.

"Steven, everyone knows where I am. I sent a picture of your lot from the map at the courthouse. No one is dead, yet. You can turn yourself over to the authorities, and get the help you need."

Porowski screamed into her face. "I thought you might replace Abigail. But I saw the way you dressed that night with your sister. You're just another whore! Like Abigail! I killed her, and I'm going to kill you." Steven pulled the trigger, and nothing happened. The hammer clicked, and that's all Wendy needed to take off running down the mountain.

He cussed, and struggled to load the clip with a fresh set of bullets. Raising the gun to shoulder height, he took his time aiming at the back of Wendy's torso. Valerie stirred, and that caused Porowski to lose concentration. He looked down at the back seat as Valerie put a hand on her swollen head.

"Oh," she groaned. When Steven looked back toward Wendy, she was gone.

"Shit," he said, and lowered the rifle.

Jennifer was close enough to hear him, and Valerie. What could she do? She needed to get to the road. The one they'd come in on. Once she had cell service, she'd call the cops. Porowski looked around as if to find a sign of some kind. He was tired, flustered, and near the end of his rope. Jennifer was on the ground, wedged into some laurel bushes. He seemed lost.

Suddenly, Steven realized he was not in control, and things seemed to be falling apart. He rubbed his head as he leaned the rifle against the rear quarter panel of the car. He looked at his hand covered in blood. The bullet had grazed his thumb, and hit a vein.

Porowski rubbed his forehead in a show of total frustration. "I'm going to kill her," he said out loud, looking at Valerie in the backseat. "Then I'm going to disappear." He climbed into the car, and when he started it, a plume of smoke shot out of the tailpipe. He backed up to the street, and Jennifer watched as he turned right, heading northwest on the twisting mountain road. Jennifer screamed into the woods.

"Wendy, get your ass up here; he's taken Valerie to go kill her."

She waited in agitation as nothing happened. Then she heard a voice off to her left, a long way from where she'd last run. "I'm coming." She circled back. Wendy was climbing over briars, and working her way around stunted black walnut, and locust trees.

Jennifer got in the car and started it; she was impatient to get going. She yelled, again. "We're losing him; come on."

Wendy ran to the car, and climbed into the passenger seat. She was out of breath. "He's," she fought to fill her lungs, "got the gun."

Jennifer was backing up as fast as she could. When she spun the wheel on the asphalt, she hit the gas, and was soon screeching tires to catch up with Porowski. "I know," she said, not taking her eyes off the road. "Call the cops when we have a signal."

Wendy held her phone up, but there was no signal. "There's nothing on the dark side of these miserable woods. There's only us, and that crazy fuck, Porowski."

Jennifer said, "He never hesitated when he saw our car; he just started shooting."

"Yeah," Wendy said, "there was no chit chat; he just wanted to kill me. I looked out the window to see who it was, and I saw he had a gun aimed at me. I moved just in time."

"I jumped out of the window. I didn't have a gun, but I couldn't leave. I just couldn't save my ass, and not look back."

"I was in the bedroom, and thought about jumping out the window. He was shooting all over the place, so I stayed on the floor."

"There!" Jennifer screamed. "Did you see that? That's blue smoke."

"Okay," Wendy said, having no idea what blue smoke meant.

"His car, Wen, it was smoking blue smoke."

"Oh, so we're close?"

"Yep," Jennifer was white-knuckling it around a corner when she saw a flash of white from the back bumper of the Taurus.

"What are we going to do once we catch up with him?" Wendy asked.

"Follow him until we have a signal." Jennifer realized that wasn't much of a plan. "Maybe," she said hesitantly, "we can have an opportunity to ram his car."

"And save the girl," Wendy smiled.

"Well," Jennifer said, closing in on the Taurus, now 20 yards in front of them. "If we don't save her, we can tell Hunter how hard we tried." The sisters burst out laughing with that one.

"Honestly," Wendy said after they laughed. "She looked like she'd been chased all night, and beaten all day."

Jennifer turned from driving to look at Wendy. "That's horrible."

"He's a sadistic psychopath that won't stop until we're all dead." Wendy was looking at the paper tag on the back of the smoking car. She glanced at her phone, but there was still no signal. "Knowing he's going to kill her should make us think about stopping him."

"I'm up for that, but all we have is mom's car, no gun, and no phone signal," Jennifer said as she had to speed up to keep up with Steven as they took a hairpin turn on another switchback.

"I think we should push him into a tree."

Chapter 17

Detective McDermott got a call from processing at the laboratory. "Shawn, I checked different spots on the pool of blood, and found no anomalies. Each section I checked had decayed red blood cells, consistent platelet coagulation, fibrin strand density constant throughout. I also ran a spectrometer, and found nothing added to the blood for preservation. I can't think of anything else to do."

The detective replied, "I got an ex-FBI private investigator telling me the blood evidence was staged. So far, he's been talking about splatter, cast-off trails, and so on. I don't want him coming back to me, and telling a story about the pool of blood."

"There's one more thing I can think to do, Shawn. I can put some samples under a microscope, and look for linear striations; that's to see if the blood has layers, and didn't come from a single incident, like a bleed out."

"How long will that take?"

"Give me ten minutes."

Shawn thought if the top man at the laboratory his police department has used for years tells him somethings fishy, he'll drop all charges on Hunter Smithfield, and put out an APB on Steven Porowski. *If I have to eat crow, and call Howard Long, I will.*

HUNTER AND LONG WERE on the phone with each other short-
ly after reading the ancestry file. Howard said, "I'll make some phone
calls. His work van was found in Burlington County. That's the same
county where the article was printed. I'm going to be working in my
car. I'm driving there, now. I'll be gathering information, and keep you
apprised. If I were you, I'd head out that way, too. We can talk by phone
during the trip, and once I have an address, I'll text it to you; otherwise,
we'll meet at a public site."

Hunter didn't have a car; his father was at the cemetery. The cops
had his vehicle impounded. He called Beverly, and asked if she had a
car at her house he could use. She said she had the keys to Jennifer's,
and Wendy's cars; they had her car. Hunter took an Uber to Beverly's
house, and on the way, they talked. She had the cabin's address. It was
a lot number on a mountain called Peach Hill. Once Hunter got into
Jennifer's car, he called Howard Long, and gave him the address. He
followed up by sending him a copy of the photo from the map in the
courthouse.

Long said, "I could use those two sisters. They've been ahead of the
game all along."

"I wouldn't rule out the mother. I think she's guided those two, and
helped point them in the right direction."

"Noted," Howard said. "I may ask her if she'd like to do a little
moonlighting as a professional snoop."

Hunter said, "I'm sure Beverly would like that. She's a recent wid-
ow, and other than babysitting the kids, I'm sure she gets bored."

Hunter punched Jennifer's car every chance he had. He was frantic
to find Valerie, and if he got his hands on Porowski, he might wring the
guy's neck.

On the ride he called his father, and told him he's free from cemetery duty. He informed him of recent developments. He told his father
he'd been doing some soul searching since all this drama first began.
He said," I'm despondent over my relationship with Jennifer ending.

Even if something happens with Valerie, our time has come, and gone. I think Jen knows it's been crumbling for several years. We'll work it out with the kids; we won't fight over them. Jennifer's not someone who holds onto grudges; she thinks that kind of thing is wrong for the soul."

Hunter's father listened without comment, and after an awkward silence, he said, "You know I always thought she was the best thing to happen with you."

"I know, dad, and that hasn't changed, not when we look back on the early years. We were in love, and living that life, but things shift, and move around, and one day, after counselors and long nights of drinking and talking, it's like we were going through the motions, staying afloat, and all that pushing through mud gets old. I honestly was not looking for someone when Valerie and I became an item. It happened, and if Jen was out and about, and working, it may have been her first."

"I read a lot of tombstones when I was killing time in the cemetery. We only get one shot. Your mom and I would have divorced ten times over if society weren't so restrictive, and divorce didn't carry such a stigma back in my time. In the end, we considered ourselves among the lucky ones. We had you, and Sarah. Both of you kids have surpassed our wildest dreams. You're both successful in your fields, and I have the best grandchildren ever made. I'll always be there for you, son."

"Thanks, dad."

MCDERMOTT GOT THE CALL from the laboratory. "I have some news, Shawn, and it's mind-boggling. I've never had to look for linear striations. But they're there. The blood was poured in layers. Like someone was emptying vials of the stuff. It was a setup. As I said, I've done this work for over 25 years, and this never came up. As a rule, no one looks for this unless pushed. "

McDermott thanked his old acquaintance, and after ending the call, his shoulders dropped. He didn't like the smell of Hunter, or the way the man conducted himself. But those things don't make a conviction. He called Howard Long, and told him he was issuing an all-points-bulletin on Steven Porowski.

"What changed your mind, detective?" Long asked.

"Blood evidence, something called linear striations."

"Most labs don't look for that," Long said.

"My guy only looked because I pushed him into it. You can tell your client the charges against him are soon to be dropped."

"I know this call wasn't easy, Detective McDermott. I know what it's like; believe me, I've been there. Just a heads up, I'm heading toward a cabin in the woods, a place inherited by Porowski on Peach Hill, in Burlington County, Lot 14. I'll keep you informed."

"I'll notify the locals," McDermott said. "You have no jurisdiction in any state, and you shouldn't be taking the law into your own hands."

"Good-bye, detective," Long said, then ended the conversation.

As it happened, Long was a resident of Virginia, and he had a concealed weapons permit. If he needed to use his gun, he wouldn't hesitate. Howard wasn't waiting for backup from law enforcement because there was a certain urgency regarding Valerie Washington. If he were a betting man, he'd put the odds of Valerie being alive somewhere near no-way, and don't count on it. And before it's all over, they needed to exhume Porowski's sister. If they did the work required in the first place, Steven would have been in jail, and none of this nonsense would be taking place.

In his experience with medical examiners, his professional opinion was they were overworked, and understaffed. That leaves room for a lot of mistakes. Howard believed there were more men in the graveyard from wives giving their overweight and overbearing husbands a little poison than anyone could guess. The examiner takes one look at the guy, sees all the organs jammed up with yellow fat, and writes down natural causes. It's not like the wife was set to inherit millions; she may be taking on debt. But she can live her remaining years without having to listen to Mr. Ass-in-the-chair barking out orders every day.

Long was passing through Reston, and approaching Dulles Airport. Soon he'd be cresting a hill, and have a beautiful vista, and in the distance, he'd get his first glimpse of the Blue Ridge Mountains. His Explorer had a radar detector set to send an alarm in time for him to slow down before it registered that he was speeding by a local cop. He was pressing 90, and was passing everything on the road. The GPS estimated an arrival time of 22 minutes. Out of habit, and tension, Howard felt his shoulder holster, and made sure the Glock 9mm, with an extended clip, was in place. It was.

Chapter 18

"Okay," Jennifer said, meaning she was going to stop him with the car. Her hands leaked buckets, and strained on the steering wheel. They came around the last curve at the base of the mountain. The road leveled, and was a straight shot toward a distant bridge over the North Shenandoah River. She glanced at the speedometer. They were traveling at 65-mph. Porowski opened up the Taurus, and a large cloud of smoke shot from the exhaust.

The roads' shoulders were crushed shale, and sloped to either side of the bridge as they quickly approached the wooden structure. Jennifer drove the right front bumper a few feet in front of Porowski's left rear quarter panel. She moved slightly right, and careened into the Taurus. He immediately lost control. He spun backward, and shot down the embankment with his windshield facing the road as he sped toward the slow-moving river. His contorted face filled the windshield in surprise, and disbelief. His eyes latched onto Wendy's as the car bounced over large rocks, some near boulder size, used for soil retention.

Jennifer slammed on her brakes, and backed up to see the Taurus flip on its top, and crush the roof, bending all the glass on the doors into fractured curves, and sending the front windshield flying from the metal frame. The car slid into the water upside down, leaving white streaks of paint on rocks, and a tormented sound like a dying, metallic animal. Jennifer swung her door open, and ran toward the vehicle, slipping on the rocks, sliding on her tailbone halfway down. Wendy was out of the passenger side, and moving with caution due to the stones, and because she knew Porowski had a rifle, and their pistol. Jennifer stood on the shore, staring into the clear water at the large rounded boulders a few inches below the waterline.

Five straight summers found Jennifer as a lifeguard at their local swimming pool when she was a high school student, and a freshman in college. She had to qualify year, after year, and if there's one thing she was proficient at, it was swimming.

Wendy stared from the shore as Jen disappeared under the water. It seemed like an eternity until she came back up. When she finally did, she had her husband's lover in tow. Valerie was at death's door. Wendy waded into the water to help Jen bring her to the rocky river bank. The girls rolled her onto her back, and pushed on her ribcage to make sure she didn't have water in her lungs.

Valerie's head tilted to the left, then she coughed out a small amount of water. It leaked from her lips as she began to breathe. The girls stood her up. She opened her eyes, and saw the two Valise sisters. An involuntary surge of emotional relief escaped from deep inside her, and she gave the girls a pitiful squeeze.

All three formed a tight, wet, and cold circle as they hugged, and wept. Wendy was crying while keeping one eye on the river for any sign of Steven. She never saw him again. They struggled to get up the stone hillside. A vehicle slammed on its breaks, and a large man came into view at the crest of the drop-off. He had a pistol in his hand, and he looked ready for battle. His big head swung from one face to another. He was holding each of their eyes for a moment. He asked, "Jennifer?" and she nodded. "Wendy?" and she also gave the nod. Then Howard Long broke into a brilliant, radiant smile. "Valerie?" It was all she could do to grunt.

Long maneuvered down the hillside, cursing, and slipping as he went. At the bottom, he picked Valerie up, and held her like a newborn. Howard clambered up to the road, and his Explorer. He used a radio attached to the dash to notify the police, and request an ambulance. Hunter screeched to a halt, shot out of his car, and ran to Valerie. As soon as she saw him, she reached out her arms, and Long gave her to Hunter. They were both crying as they waited for an ambulance.

In the waiting room of the hospital, everyone gave their statement. It ended with Howard and Hunter describing the empty house in the woods. With nothing else to go on, they both concluded to drive in the opposite direction. They'd hoped to find something, any sign. A search by the local police was called, and organized, to find Porowski. A few hours later, Shawn McDermott showed up, and wrote a report. He gave Hunter a sincere apology, one that felt real, and Hunter accepted it because Valerie was safe. She'd need two days to recover in the hospital. There was no sexual assault, but she could probably use the tools a skilled therapist has to help build back trust in her fellow man.

STEVEN POROWSKI CLAMORED up the far shore, wincing as he grabbed onto laurel branches to hoist himself up the steep hillside. His hand throbbed, and his nose ached. He was careful not to break any branches, and leave a sign for those who would follow. He was wet, cold, and defeated. His mind was reeling. How could those two sisters track him down? It meant he wasn't as smart as he thought he was. It was humbling, and he understood that he had severe limitations. That opinion was thrust upon him when a river began pouring into his get-away car.

He had his wallet, and all his bank routing numbers for the various accounts set up around Slate Shore. He could get enough funds to start over somewhere, and if he strived for what he had once dreamed of having with Abigail, a family and children, it would be prudent of him never to forget that he was chased down, and beaten by three, average women. One escaped, and two tracked him down, and nearly killed him. If he didn't transfer all the hate and anger he had toward Abigail onto other women, he may be able to save his future.

The homes on this side of the river were mostly vacation cabins. There was very little industry, or employment in this rural part of Virginia. Porowski found an open window, and soon had dry clothes on. There was a four-wheeler under a tarp by a stack of cut firewood. He got it started, and took some gravel roads to the base of the foothill. At a convenience store, slash old house with a gas pump in front, Steven used the phone to call for an Uber driver. It was wishful thinking that a driver existed in this neck of the woods. But, they're everywhere.

Soon, a driver showed up in a relatively new Nissan Pathfinder, and whisked him away. In Winchester, he found a Greyhound bus station. He was able to pay for a ticket through PayPal. As the first of the searchers scanned the river banks, Steven closed his eyes, and napped on his way to New York. It was only a matter of weeks before Porowski became David Lewis Archer, complete with a new I.D.

Porowski realized he'd begun hoarding soon after he'd killed Abigail. It was his way of never losing anything again. He was self-aware of his misplaced anger. It was like the hoarding was a reaction to events that were long gone, and having nothing to do with his present life. Steven consumed psychology books of every size, and depth, in his off time from working in a computer repair shop. He was slowly, methodically, convincing himself that he could live an average life, and eventually have a wife, and children.

Without the release, and the expertise of a trained therapist, Steven was stuffing down many emotions, swallowing a lifetime of pain, and it would only be a matter of time until he acted out on his anger. But he'd be smarter than the man that crawled onto the banks of the North Shenandoah, soaking wet, and defeated by a group of women. On and off, Porowski was plagued about how those women tracked him down. With caution that vibrated at a fever pitch, and every move made like a chess master, he operated like a jewel thief.

As of January, in the United States, there are an estimated 2000 serial killers. And a quarter of a million deaths go unsolved. Steven Porowski, a.k.a., David Archer, joined those ranks with his third kill. Look in the back of his sock drawer, in the right-hand corner. A blue, antique sapphire necklace rests patiently for the next trophy.

HOWARD LONG FILLED out the employment form with Beverly Valise. He thought she'd be a great asset to the Marks & Hammel detective agency. But, more importantly, he believed she'd be good company on a Saturday night for dinner, and perhaps a movie. And, she was pleased with his request. She loved her husband, in life, and death. She also cared very much about Beverly Valise, and her present life, and a strong desire to live – like her grandchildren said, "Do it like you mean it, Grandma."

Wendy wrote Ray Thomas, the love of her life, a letter. She told him about her ordeal with Porowski, and all the excitement, and terror in that episode. The incident made her realize what not paying attention to their relationship had cost. She had a few tears when she licked the stamp, and mailed the envelope.

Three weeks later, babysitting Olivia and Drake, on a Saturday night, while Beverly and Jennifer were on dates with Howard and Marshal, respectively, she got a call. It was a familiar number, and she and Ray talked until the sun rose Sunday morning.

THE END

Printed in Great Britain
by Amazon